W9-CEY-215

Dear Reader,

Do *you* have a secret fantasy? Everybody does. Maybe it's to be rich and famous and beautiful. Or to start a no-strings affair with a sexy mysterious stranger. Or to have a sizzling second chance with a former sweetheart.... You'll find these dreams—and much more—in Temptation's exciting new yearlong promotion, Secret Fantasies.

Popular author Janice Kaiser has written a dynamite story about a heroine who's not afraid to fantasize. But Darien is in for a *surprise* when her "fantasy man" comes to life! Enjoy all the sensual delights of *Night Games*.

In the coming months, look for Secret Fantasies books by Lisa Harris, Regan Forest and JoAnn Ross. Please write and let us know how you enjoy the "fantasy."

Happy Reading!

The Editors

c/o Harlequin Temptation
225 Duncan Mill Road
Don Mills, Ontario
Canada M3B 3K9

Dear Reader,

Birthdays are a special time for making wishes and dreaming. Yet the thought that a dream or fantasy might actually come true can be scary. For most of us, it's safer to keep a secret wish locked safely in our heart, rather than risk disappointment.

My heroine in *Night Games,* Darien Hughes, is celebrating her thirtieth birthday when she spots a special man across a crowded room—exactly the kind of man she thinks would make a perfect lover. Darien, who writes for a newspaper, lets her imagination run free, and shares with her readers a list of all the wonderful and exciting things her fantasy lover would do for her…if he came into her life. And then, to her surprise, he does appear at her desk, offering to make her every wish come true.

At first, Darien's afraid to accept his challenge. But her fantasy man is so sexy, so charming, that she knows she'll never forgive herself if she doesn't find out what will happen. Soon she is off on the biggest adventure of her life. And before it is over, she'll risk everything— even her safety—to find love with a perfect stranger.

Writing *Night Games* made me think about my own dreams—especially one I had eleven years ago when I gave up practicing law and started turning my daydreams into novels. I have never regretted taking that risk, and I hope Darien's story encourages you to risk making your dreams become realities, too.

Sincerely,

Janice Kaiser

He was a fantasy come to life

Darien stepped into his arms. Sam felt warm and alive. She ran her palm over his bare chest, marveling that the mat of hair was silky rather than crinkly. Being in his arms was bliss. He seemed to be muscle and bone and flesh, smooth and hard, all at the same time.

Sam nibbled his way up her neck to her ear. At the same time his thumbs stroked her nipples through the silk of the dress. She let out a tiny groan of pleasure.

His lips found hers. And when the long kiss finally ended, she pulled away to look into Sam's eyes. They were dark with passion. And the yearning she saw reflected in them mirrored her own feelings.

This was no game of fantasy. This was real....

Janice Kaiser loved writing about fantasy in her latest Temptation, *Night Games.* "Fantasy is a vital part of any good relationship," she asserts. "And definitely a fun subject to explore!" One of Janice's own fantasies comes to life this month. *Private Sins,* her first mainstream title for Mira Books—a Harlequin imprint—will be published. Look for it in March 1995 at your local bookstores!

Books by Janice Kaiser

HARLEQUIN TEMPTATION
466—DECEPTIONS
477—WILD LIKE THE WIND
508—STAR

HARLEQUIN SUPERROMANCE
494—THE BIG SECRET
541—CRADLE OF DREAMS
597—THE YANQUI PRINCE

Don't miss any of our special offers. Write to us at the following address for information on our newest releases.

Harlequin Reader Service
U.S.: 3010 Walden Ave., P.O. Box 1325, Buffalo, NY 14269
Canadian: P.O. Box 609, Fort Erie, Ont. L2A 5X3

NIGHT GAMES
JANICE KAISER

Harlequin Books

TORONTO • NEW YORK • LONDON
AMSTERDAM • PARIS • SYDNEY • HAMBURG
STOCKHOLM • ATHENS • TOKYO • MILAN
MADRID • WARSAW • BUDAPEST • AUCKLAND

For Melissa Krum,
with love

ISBN 0-373-25630-2

NIGHT GAMES

Copyright © 1995 by Belles Lettres, Inc.

This edition published by arrangement with Harlequin Enterprises B.V.

® and TM are trademarks of the publisher. Trademarks indicated with ® are registered in the United States Patent and Trademark Office, the Canadian Trade Marks Office and in other countries.

Printed in U.S.A.

1

"Bob, tell me the truth," Darien Hughes said, "is this a warning? Are you saying if I don't improve, I'm out of here?"

Bob Smits turned from the dirty window of his cramped office overlooking Battery Street. "Darien, I'm *not* about to fire you, and this is *not* a warning. I admire your work. You know that."

"But you aren't satisfied with it. Is that it?"

"You've done some excellent pieces for the *Bulletin*," he said. "You have talent, but . . ."

She waited nervously. Whatever followed the *but* was the point Bob wanted to make. She watched, trying hard to remain calm.

"But . . . you can do even better."

"Please. Just tell me what's wrong, exactly. What is it that you don't like?"

Bob Smits, feature editor of the *San Francisco Bulletin*, stepped over to where she was sitting and dropped his large frame onto the corner of his old wood desk. His eyes were sympathetic. She hoped that was a good sign.

"Darien, sometimes your writing lacks passion. For example, the piece you did on friendships between gay men and straight women. It was thoughtful, thorough, but it lacked . . . I don't know . . . fire, I suppose. You didn't let yourself go, dig into the emotion of the subject. You just observed, and in so doing, you held back."

Darien knew he was right. She'd felt as if she was walking on ice while writing that particular article. "I understand what you're saying," she said.

"If a subject bothers you, it's better not to write about it—unless, of course, your sensitivity about that subject is what you want to explore."

Darien lowered her head, embarrassed at having let him down. Taking risks, exposing herself emotionally, was hard for her. It always had been. That had been okay, though, because it hadn't affected her work. Until now.

Bob Smits had seen a series of articles she'd done on life in Greenwich Village for the *New York Post*. He'd flown east to see her, insisting she had to come to California to write for the *Bulletin*. As a brand-new paper taking on the *Chronicle* and the *Examiner*, the *Bulletin* had to deliver something different to survive. Roger Gilbert, the publisher, had targeted the young professional set, hoping to win an enthusiastic following in a couple of key niche markets and then build the readership from there. The features department was, in Gilbert's scheme, key. She had a fabulous opportunity to shine, and here she was, blowing it.

Smits leaned forward and gave her a fatherly pat on the shoulder. "You're good," he said, "and you can be even better. Remember, it isn't always enough to inform. You've got to excite the reader, as well."

Darien nodded, but had trouble looking him in the eye. She felt dreadful, not to mention embarrassed. Bob had gone to bat for her, and she'd let him down. "I'll do my best."

He drew a breath and sighed, evidently glad to have the worst of their little chat behind him. "Listen, I appreciate you coming in on a Saturday. I didn't want to have this conversation in the middle of one of our usual hectic days."

"No problem, Bob."

"It's beautiful out, why don't you drive out to the beach and let the ocean breezes clear your head? Refresh yourself and come back Monday morning bright-eyed and bushy-tailed."

"A friend is taking me to lunch over in Marin," she said. "To some place called Sam's."

"Good for you. Sam's is a great place to hang out on a weekend. Janet and I usually make it over to Tiburon at least once each summer. Special occasion?"

Darien nodded, still feeling humiliated, but doing her best to bear up. "Yes, it's my birthday."

Bob Smits's mouth fell. "Oh, geez. I'm sorry, Darien. If I'd known I wouldn't have dragged you down here. You should have said something. This could have waited."

"It's all right, Bob. No big deal. I'm glad we talked."

"Well, listen, I don't want to keep you. Go on up to Marin and have fun. And don't worry. New job, new town. There are always wrinkles to iron out."

Darien nodded again and got to her feet. She felt awkward, partly because he did. That was proof their friendly chat had been dead serious. "Thanks for giving me a chance to improve," she said. "I understand what you want now, and I'll do better. I promise."

Darien couldn't get out of the office fast enough. Once she got into the hall, she hurried to the elevator almost at a run. As she stood waiting for the car to arrive, waves of self-doubt buffeted her. That was the worst thing about a setback like this—it took guts and a lot of energy to get up off the floor and charge back into the fray. But that's exactly what she had to do. She had to summon her courage, get her creative juices flowing. Her future might well depend on it.

"YOU'RE PROBABLY making more of it than is justified," Maryanne said as the wind rushed past. They were in her ancient Mustang convertible, driving along the Redwood Highway in Marin, the July sun beating down on them. "If you were in serious trouble, he'd have handed you your walking papers."

"Maybe," Darien said. "But Bob was right. For some reason I haven't found my stride."

"At least he acknowledged a period of adjustment is required. Everyone needs to get used to a new town."

"I'm not so sure. A good writer ought to be able to work well anywhere, under any conditions. Still, it was nice of him to give me an excuse. But still, the point is I've got to start producing. I need a whiz-bang idea, something I can really sink my teeth into. And I need it fast."

"I have confidence in you, Darien. You're going to be the talk of the town. Just wait and see."

Maryanne Patterson was great. They'd become close during the six months Darien had been in San Francisco. One of her very first assignments had been an article on the lot of professional women in the city. During interviews, Maryanne's name had come up so often that Darien had wanted to meet her. They'd hit it off from the start.

Maryanne was a psychologist, specializing in the personal and work-related problems of professional women. Darien liked her a lot. Maryanne was warm and funny and a little crazy. She was a good listener, too, which was hardly surprising considering her profession, but she didn't insist on analyzing her friends. Mostly she accepted them as they were, though there were times when she'd slip into a therapy mode.

"Why don't you put it out of your mind and try to relax," Maryanne said over the roar of the wind. "Monday will come soon enough. Besides, this is a special birthday, and you're supposed to enjoy it."

"I haven't given it all that much thought, if you want to know the truth. Turning thirty's no big deal."

"*Every* birthday is a big deal, and this one's a milestone. A new decade!"

Maryanne was trying to be upbeat, and she appreciated it. As Darien tucked a strand of dark hair under her scarf, she glanced at her friend. As usual, Maryanne was wearing a funky hat—she adored unusual things and got most of her accessories at antique shops or secondhand clothing stores. Today she had smashed an old-fashioned green wool beret that had been new in the forties down over her ears. Even so, her strawberry curls hung out the back of the hat and were flying in the wind.

"I hope you like champagne," Maryanne said, "because there's no better way to turn thirty than sipping some primo bubbly and watching men."

"If you say so."

Now that they were through the tunnel and descending toward Richardson Bay, Darien felt the warmth of the sun. It was at least ten degrees hotter than it had been on the other side of the Golden Gate. In fact, the trees lining Park Presidio Boulevard, close to where Maryanne's flat was, had been shrouded in a thin layer of fog—so thin that the gauzy sun still managed to cast shadows.

San Francisco's weather was schizophrenic in summer. Darien doubted she'd ever get used to it. At her bus stop, some people wore T-shirts while others had on wool coats. Early on, she'd decided to always carry a sweater.

But Maryanne had insisted that Sam's was terribly Mediterranean, so Darien had dressed accordingly, putting on a yellow sleeveless cotton T-shirt dress that had been a holdover from her New York days.

Darien wasn't quite sure why Maryanne insisted that they go to Sausalito to celebrate, unless it was the offhand remark she'd made a few weeks earlier about associating her birthday with hot weather and the ocean. Her family had spent their summers on Cape Cod, in the same cottage they rented each year. Her birthdays on the Cape were a special family tradition—one of the few in which she had center stage. She treasured the memories of each and every one of them.

Maryanne turned on the radio, punching buttons—just long enough to hear a couple of bars of music—before switching it off.

"So tell me, what did you do on *your* thirtieth?" Darien asked. "It was so *long* before I moved out here that any gossip about it has long since faded away."

Maryanne bared her teeth and silently mouthed the word *bitch*.

Darien laughed.

"If you must know, I stayed home and cried," Maryanne replied. "And not because I'd become an old lady. The guy I'd been dating at the time, somebody named Fred, as I recall, dumped me the night before."

"The night before your *birthday?*"

Maryanne pulled her beret farther down on her forehead and nodded. "Can you think of a better time?"

"That's terrible. Men can be so heartless."

"True. But we love them anyway. Besides, my dear, the real trick is to not let your happiness depend on what *they* do, only what *you* do."

Darien slowly nodded. "You know something? I think you may be right about that."

At the Tiburon Boulevard exit they left the freeway, following the road along the water's edge. Darien looked out at the bay, recalling the drives along the shore of Nantucket Sound—the sailboats and the smell of salt water. A feeling of nostalgia went through her, and she actually felt twinges of homesickness.

She'd been sentimental all day. Her parents hadn't called to wish her a happy birthday. The only other time they'd missed since she'd left home was the summer she'd toured Europe and they hadn't been able to get through. But she'd ended up talking to them that night.

Her parents were both college professors and were extremely close to one another. In fact they'd been so devoted that Darien had always felt like a third wheel around them. She'd been born relatively late in their lives, after a number of years of marriage, and she hadn't been planned. Not that she was ever neglected or mistreated, of course, but there was never any doubt in her mind that they didn't need her to be happy. Far and away the most important person in each of their lives was the other.

But that was ancient history. Except for the birthday calls and occasional holiday visits, she led a separate existence from her parents. She was thirty now, on her own, getting jobs—and maybe losing them—making her own way, regardless. There was certainly nothing to be gained by looking back on her childhood. And she rarely did—except on days like this. Birthdays.

"Speaking of men," Maryanne said, "what happened with the sales rep you went out with a few weeks ago? What was his name?"

"Alan Maybank."

"Yeah, Alan. Didn't that work out? I haven't heard you talk about him in a while."

"No, he was the same as all the rest. All he wanted was to go to bed with me. He wasn't obnoxious about it or anything, but he made it pretty clear where he was headed. And I let him know I wasn't interested in going there."

"You sort of had hopes for him, didn't you?"

"Not really," Darien said with a sigh. "I've been cynical about the single life since . . ." She faltered, feeling a sudden, unexpected rush of emotion. It happened like that every so often—when she remembered—though less and less with each passing year. She turned to look out at the bay, but Maryanne noticed.

"Todd?"

Darien nodded. "Yes, but I don't think I want to get into that, if you don't mind. Not today. Not now."

"I understand."

And Darien knew she did.

Maryanne slowed the car as they entered the village. "This is Tiburon," she said. "Let's find a place to park and see what kind of trouble we can find." She pulled into the municipal lot. "Promise me you'll drink most of the champagne, though. I've got to drive home."

"All right," Darien said. "I'll drink and you can watch the men. Just give me your word there'll be no waiters singing happy birthday while I have to stare at a cupcake with a candle stuck in it."

"At Sam's? Are you kidding? This place has class."

"Good. I've had all the humiliation I can handle in one day."

THE TOWN, Darien noted, was built on the tip of a peninsula that poked out into the bay. Angel Island, a hilly, golden jewel preserved in its natural state, sat offshore. Belvedere Island, known for its walled mansions and lush gardens, abutted Tiburon to the west. Between them there was a sparkling view of the San Francisco skyline in the distance—a city of whites and pastels lying beneath a pale sky. The blue-gray waters of the bay were studded with sailboats, moving like feathers over a pond.

Sam's was located in the middle of a long row of quaint waterfront buildings. As Darien walked through the bar and main dining room she concluded that the restaurant itself looked kind of ordinary, not unlike a lot of seafood places back east. But a single glimpse of the deck was all it took for her to understand what drew people to Sam's.

The deck was built on huge pilings and jutted into the protected cove. From where she stood, she saw people eating pasta or seafood, drinking a bottle of wine or an imported beer, as sea gulls soared overhead. There was a relaxed energy about the place—more reminiscent of Portofino or Antibes or even the Cape than New York.

Outdoor energy in the summer was special. Sun-drenched was not New York, which drew its strength from the night. Tiburon, Darien discovered, was closer to an easterner's common conception of California than was San Francisco with its cool breezes and fog.

While they waited for the maître d', a guy in a polo shirt and sun-bleached hair, to figure out what to do with them, Darien glanced around. A flotilla of pleasure craft was moored at the surrounding docks, giving Sam's a yacht-club feel. Yet there was nothing snobby about the place. Jeans and tank tops mixed easily with the silk, the pearls and the gold watches.

Despite the crowd, Maryanne got them a table after only a ten-minute wait. If a bill passed hands, Darien didn't see it. To the questioning glares of others who'd been there longer, they were led to a table in the center of the deck. Maryanne asked for champagne first thing.

"How did you do that?" Darien asked under her breath.

"I had reservations," Maryanne replied.

"Do they take them?"

"Not exactly." And that was all she said.

Darien inhaled the salt air, listened to the chatter—not all of it in English. Two French couples at a nearby table were engaged in an animated discussion, but they were speaking too fast for her to pick up more than an occasional word. On the other side a rather debonair man with white hair and a neatly trimmed beard was talking in seductive tones to a buxom blonde thirty years his junior. A gay couple in their forties seated behind them was unabashedly discussing the food in loud enough tones for everyone around them to hear—and presumably appreciate. Darien had already learned that in California, like France, one talked a great deal about food.

Maryanne began discussing the menu just as someone seated near the water tossed scraps of bread into the air. Instantly a flock of cawing, fluttering gulls began competing for the food. Darien glanced over to observe the aerial battle and, in doing so, saw him.

He was seated alone at a small table in the corner of the deck, next to the railing. He was remarkably good-looking. He had brownish blond hair, slightly wind-blown, and he was dressed in jeans and a white linen shirt that had most likely set him back a couple of hundred dollars. He had on lightly tinted glasses, and his gold watch sparkled in the sun. He was probably in his mid-thirties. The atmosphere all around him was convivial and alive, yet he sat thoughtfully, as if oblivious to his surroundings, looking off, the index finger of one hand against his cheek.

Darien let her imagination go. She judged he was either waiting for someone or thinking about someone. She probably was projecting, especially given the fact she had no way of knowing a thing about him, but she was almost certain that she sensed a loneliness in him that was not unlike her own. Was she identifying with him?

She checked and saw that the other place at his table had been cleared. So he was definitely dining alone. A remarkably handsome man, drinking wine on the deck at Sam's on a Saturday afternoon in July. What circumstances prompted him to be there?

Maryanne, who suddenly discovered she was talking to the wind, leaned over to see what she was looking at. "Mmm, I was wondering what had gotten your attention." She nodded. "Not bad." Then, laughing, she said, "I told you the man-watching was good here. But normally they aren't alone. This is more a place to enjoy the ambience than to actually meet someone." She stared at the guy a moment longer. "Looking at him makes you curious why he doesn't have a date. Or a wife."

Darien studied him. "It doesn't look like he's wearing a ring, but that doesn't guarantee anything."

"Even if he's not married, he might have a woman and two or three kids at home. Especially in this day and age."

Darien studied him some more, then shook her head. "I don't think so. This isn't a day out of the house for him. He's a bachelor. I'd bet on it."

"What makes you so sure?" Maryanne asked.

"He has that predatory look about him."

"Predatory?"

"A man on the prowl. Well, what do *you* see, Dr. Freud?"

"I don't see a predator," Maryanne said. "In fact, he looks oblivious to his surroundings to me. If he was on the make, he'd be eyeing every woman in the place."

"Like we're eyeing him?"

Maryanne gave Darien a quirky smile. "We're professionals. We evaluate people for a living, remember? We're almost *obliged* to be doing this."

Darien laughed, shaking her head. "Patterson, sometimes you're too much."

They continued to check the guy out in silence. He was gorgeous, no denying that. Darien was fascinated by him. The predator quality was subtle, carefully masked, but she was aware of it. He had to know that half the women there had been looking at him.

Darien was no stranger to the phenomenon. She wasn't an exceptional beauty, but she knew she had a certain charisma that drew men to her. She had a good figure, long legs and the kind of beauty that was more distinctive than classic. Soon after arriving in San Francisco she'd had a makeover, and the woman who did it said she had an interesting, unusual face that radiated intelligence and character. Darien took it with a grain of salt, but she knew she had great eyes. They were a pale, pale blue with heavy dark lashes. Her eyes were her best feature. Todd had worshiped them.

"Be honest, wouldn't you like to meet him?" Maryanne asked. "In my heart of hearts, I know he's probably an arrogant, self-centered Lothario who exploits women and sucks the lifeblood out of them, but doesn't a part of you want to find out?"

"No," Darien said, "not really."

"Oh, come on. I didn't say go to bed with him or even let him buy you a drink. I said *talk* to him, just to confirm or deny all the awful things you suspect."

Darien shook her head. "That's not what pops into my mind when I see a guy like that."

"What does?"

"Honestly, I don't want to find out what he's really like. It's more satisfying to indulge myself with the fantasy. I can't get hurt that way and, as an extra bonus, I'm the one in charge."

Maryanne screwed up her face. "Well, *I'm* certainly not ashamed to admit that I'd like to get to know him better."

The waitress came with the champagne, drawing their attention to their celebration. Maryanne took half a glass, reminding Darien she'd have to do the drinking for both of them.

Darien picked up her wineglass. "Shall we drink to spinsterhood and the joys of sexual fantasy?"

"No, we're going to put the best possible spin on this. Here's to a fabulous new decade, kiddo. May you prosper in your work and end up deliriously happy with, say, somebody incredibly delicious like Mr. Wonderful over there."

Darien laughed. "I'd settle for a good idea for a feature article."

They touched glasses and each took a sip of their wine. Darien looked up at the cloudless sky, feeling a momentary joy, albeit a fragile one.

The waitress took their orders. The gay couple paid their bill and left. Soon after that the French group departed, too. But the aging Don Juan next to them continued to coo into his young friend's ear, eliciting an occasional chortle and lots of leg crossing and posturing. The woman seemed to like it when he took her fingers and kissed them.

Darien's gaze kept wandering to the guy seated by the railing. It was surprisingly pleasurable just to look at him.

He continued to maintain the same thoughtful, preoccupied demeanor, even when the waiter arrived with his lunch. Darien was completely absorbed by him. Before long she found herself staring unabashedly. And to her utter amazement she started to feel lusty—at least she assumed that's what the twinges inside her meant.

She began imagining herself sitting across from him, and the way he'd take her hand. He would be more subtle and sincere than the over-the-hill rake with the blonde. And he would, of course, truly adore her. He'd be a fabulous and attentive lover—none of this selfishness that was so common in other men. Sensitive, caring, devoted. Ah, a fantasy, indeed.

When she turned from him, she saw that Maryanne was watching her, a big smile spread across her face. Darien blushed.

"That must have been some daydream. Sure you don't want to send over a bottle of wine with your phone number?"

"Shut up, Patterson."

"At least we know you're a normal red-blooded American girl."

"My fantasy life has always been healthy," Darien said.

They both laughed. Darien had another sip of champagne, her eyes gliding again to the mystery man.

As she watched, he swirled the wine in his glass and then drank. This was a man with class and sophistication, a man who used his body well, a man resonating with sensuality. If she had to guess, she'd say he was an accomplished lover.

What was really interesting, perhaps even more so than the man himself, was the effect he was having on her. She knew it was her state of mind—the occasion and the champagne—but something about him had really grabbed her. Guys, even handsome ones, normally didn't affect her that way. This one was special.

"Tempted?" Maryanne asked, reading her thoughts.

"The illusion is wonderful, I admit—or maybe I should say, the *delusion*. But no, I'm not tempted. Not really. I wouldn't want to destroy the fantasy by acting on it."

"Why? Because you're afraid of him, or afraid of yourself?"

Darien grimaced. "Can't forget you're a shrink, can you?"

Maryanne winked. "I'm enjoying this as much as you, kiddo. Vicarious thrills aren't all bad, you know."

Darien took a long sip of champagne, and as she did, it hit her. Her eyes rounded and she put down the glass. "Maryanne! That's it!"

"What's it?"

"My article. You just gave me the perfect idea for my article."

Maryanne frowned. "What are you talking about?"

"You said you were enjoying this every bit as much as I am. Well, if my secret fantasies appeal to you, they'll appeal to my readers."

"You're going to write an article about your secret fantasies?"

"About this incident. About what I'm feeling right now. Bob told me to put passion in my writing. What could be better than this...him?" She looked at her poor, unsuspecting prey.

"I think you've had too much champagne."

"No, it's a wonderful idea. I know it is." Darien felt so excited she wanted to go over and give Mr. Wonderful a great big hug. Unknowingly, he could have saved her job.

"You're serious, aren't you?"

"Of course." Darien fidgeted in her chair. She drank some more wine. Then she gazed at her fantasy lover, thinking of ways to express in an article what she was feeling. "Yes," she said as much to herself as to Maryanne, "this is good. This is very good. It will work."

"Well, I'm glad you're happy. What happens next? Do you go over and talk to him?"

"No," Darien said, "I don't think so. It's my fantasy that's important, not him. He doesn't matter any more than a movie star up on the screen. It's only what I do with him in my mind that counts."

"Need I remind you that you write for a family newspaper?"

Darien chuckled. "My article doesn't have to be X-rated to be interesting."

"I admit you've captured my imagination."

"You see!" She rubbed her hands together. "This is going to be great, Maryanne, just great."

FIFTEEN MINUTES LATER they were eating shrimp salads, and Darien was plotting out her article in detail, thinking she might even write a series if everything worked out well. Every once in a while she'd break from her reverie long enough to say something to Maryanne, but mostly she thought about the man of her dreams, who was looking better and better by the minute.

"I still think you ought to go talk to him. Once he leaves, your chance will be gone," Maryanne said.

"I couldn't," she insisted. "It'd ruin everything. Right now he's perfect. I've got to keep him that way."

Maryanne screwed up her face, the way she did when she was perplexed. "One of us is unclear on the concept. Is it me?"

"No, it's just that you're thinking like a woman, and I'm thinking like a writer. Which, my friend, is exactly why I want to keep him where I can control him, in my fantasies."

"But what if you met the guy and actually liked him?"

"Odds are against it. Anyway, I'm trying to save my career, not start a family."

Maryanne almost choked on a bite of salad. "I guess it's me who's unclear on the concept, then. The solution, I suppose, is to read your article."

Darien was feeling quite good now. She didn't care that she was thirty years old today, or that she'd been lazing around in the sunshine talking about sex with another woman while the most gorgeous man she'd ever laid eyes on remained oblivious to her existence. None of that mattered because she was onto an angle for a story—an inspired, creative angle that could save her tail feathers.

"Uh-oh," Maryanne said.

"What?"

"Your dreamboat is leaving."

Darien turned and saw her hero getting to his feet. She studied his body, the graceful way he moved. She cemented his near-perfect features into her brain. Her heart began to race as she watched him make his way around the deck. Anyone watching might have thought she was leering, but she wasn't. She was making him a prisoner in her imagination. When he disappeared from sight,

Darien slowly let the air from her lungs, wondering if she looked half as spent as she felt.

"Is that sad or what?" Maryanne said. "Your birthday fantasy just walked right out of your life, never to be seen again."

Darien shrugged. "I can live with that. If my article touches my readers half as much as you've been touched just by witnessing this, then I'll be way ahead of the game."

"But . . ."

"Sometimes, Maryanne, dreams truly are better than reality. Besides, this is business."

"There's a needy woman behind that philosophy," Maryanne said. "Don't neglect her, Darien. Please, don't neglect her. That's all I'm going to say."

"Don't cry for me," she said, taking a drink of champagne. "I didn't want *him*. Not really. What I wanted, I got."

"Then I guess we can consider it a successful birthday."

Darien nodded. "Yes, it was, thanks to you."

"Oh, don't thank me. The fantasy was in *your* head. All I did was supply the setting. And the bubbly."

2

THE FOLLOWING THURSDAY Darien arrived at her office around eleven. There was a vase of long-stemmed red roses and a note from Bob Smits on her desk. "It takes guts to write from the heart, to bare the soul. But when it works, it works," he'd written. "Congratulations."

She glanced around to make sure nobody was watching her, then leaned over to sniff a bud. The scent was heavenly, but the endorsement gave her the most joy. Evidently, her fantasies had turned Bob on—journalistically speaking, of course—and she couldn't be happier.

She plopped into her chair, taking comfort in the familiar energy of the newsroom—the clatter of keyboards, the ringing of phones, the spirited conversations. Everybody's cubicle was their womb, the place where they could draw into themselves to work.

She glanced at the cardboard box on the floor next to her desk. There'd been eight or ten letters in it on Wednesday, but it was half full now. The initial responses from readers had been, for the most part, laudatory. She had gotten letters from both men and women. Two guys had even sent along pictures of themselves. One man had proposed marriage.

There had been numerous calls, as well. After the first eight or nine, she'd asked the receptionist, Virginia, to screen them. No sense overloading her voice mail. Already there was a fresh stack of twenty-five or thirty phone message slips on her cluttered desk. She randomly shuffled through them, confirming they were more of the same.

To save time, Virginia had taken to coding the messages. *Lunch* or *drinks* meant the caller wanted to take Darien out, *love* meant he wanted to express his admiration. The women callers fell mostly into a single category, which Virginia had designated *sister.* That meant they identified with her, shared her viewpoint and were grateful for her putting into words what they'd been thinking or feeling for years.

The negative callers rarely left a name or phone number, so Virginia had taken to marking them on a tally sheet. They fell into two categories—obscene calls, coded X, and the morally indignant responses, coded either *disgusted* or *slut*, depending on the caller's degree of outrage.

There was no disputing that she'd aroused passions. That gratified her—especially after what Bob had said. Inciting people to think and feel was a prime objective of journalism. It also sold newspapers, which would raise her stock with Mr. Gilbert and the editorial staff.

Pleased as she was by the response, Darien had found the past few days draining. She'd been riding an emotional roller coaster beginning the night she'd gotten home from Tiburon. "Sam," as she'd named the guy who'd inspired her fantasies, had turned out to be much more than an idea for a story—he'd become a minor obsession.

At first she'd let her imagination wander. The way she figured it, the richer her fantasies were, the more material she'd have to draw on. After all, the objective of her piece wasn't simply to recount her make-believe adventures, but rather to evaluate and explore what effect her fantasy sex life had on her. Sam was key. Just any guy—even another good-looking one—wouldn't do because the very best fantasies required someone who sparked the imagination, set the juices flowing. And that guy on the deck at Sam's had really done it for her.

During the ride home that afternoon, she had put her head back, closed her eyes, let the wind caress her and imagined it was Sam at the wheel of the Mustang convertible, not Maryanne. They could have been headed off somewhere for a sexy weekend or a candlelit evening at his apartment or to the latest dance club. The possibilities were legion. And for some reason, she found that she wanted to explore them all, every last one of them.

It didn't sink in how much her game had gotten to her until she awoke in the middle of the night after dreaming about making love with Sam. That shouldn't have been surprising, considering she'd salted her unconscious by thinking about him all evening. In fact, she'd gotten so involved in inventing a persona for him that her parents' phone call just after dinner had almost seemed an imposition.

She hadn't told them what was going on, of course. They never discussed that sort of thing. The closest her parents ever came to getting personal was to occasionally ask about her work. And even when that happened, they usually just listened before giving a polite response.

After her father had wished her happy birthday he'd gotten off the phone and her mother brought her up to date on what had been going on in their lives. Then, uncharacteristically, her mother had asked if she had anyone special in her life. The question had been ironic, considering.

"I've dated some, Mother," she'd said, "but there's no one in particular."

A moment of silence followed, then her mother said, "There was a time when a girl worried about turning thirty without a husband on the horizon, though I know that's changed. Still, dear, your father and I wonder if you aren't avoiding commitment because of what happened. We hate to think the past is standing in the way of your happiness."

Darien was touched to think they cared enough to worry about her that way. She knew they weren't indifferent to her happiness, but to reach out after all this time was unexpected.

Still, the way her mother had handled it was vintage Alice Hughes. From the time of Todd's death, she'd been reluctant to address the situation directly, preferring to talk around the subject. "What happened" or "your tragedy" were the ways she tended to refer to it.

"Sounds like my thirtieth birthday is bothering you more than it is me, Mother," she said.

"Daddy and I are concerned for you, Darien. We always have been. I suppose we expected that by now you'd have settled down with a family of your own."

"Surely I'm not an emotional burden," she'd replied, realizing too late the remark came off a bit more sarcastically than she'd intended.

Her mother had let it pass, being one to avoid emotional confrontations at any cost. "Your father and I brought you up to be independent," she said calmly, "and we've always been pleased that you were. And proud."

Darien hadn't doubted that. But there had been times when she'd wished they'd been more willing to demonstrate their love. They'd always seemed to dole it out judiciously, like a teacher reluctant to bestow too much praise on a student.

But she'd learned years ago that there was nothing to be gained from crying over the trials and tribulations of childhood. She loved her parents, and they loved her...in their way. She'd long since decided to deal with them on their terms, and for the most part she had been successful.

"Hey, it's the queen of the hop" came a voice from behind her.

Darien turned to see Rod Barker, the *Bulletin*'s main sports writer, standing at the entrance to her cubicle. A large, hefty man in his early thirties, Rod was in one of his saggy brown sports jackets and faded jeans, his favored uniform. He had a big grin on his face.

"I hear you're a hot date these days. Had any good offers for the weekend?" He was a tease—the sort that had a knack for taking things a step too far.

"A few," she replied. "But if you're looking for sexual stimulation, Rod, you're welcome to open my mail."

He chuckled. "Write about sex, you're sure to get mail."

"That hardly was my intent," she said dryly.

"Maybe, but you certainly managed to get some attention. Last night after the game I had a few of the Giants asking me what you look like."

"What did you tell them?"

"That you're a knockout, of course," he said with a grin. "I can fix you up with a utility infielder, a starting outfielder or a pitcher whenever you want. Two of them are even single."

She rolled her eyes. "Thanks, Rod, I'll let you know."

He gave her a wink and went off.

Darien took one of the envelopes from the box and idly opened it. She wasn't so sure she liked the kind of celebrity that was coming with this article. Inciting passions was one thing, evoking lust was another.

The letter in her hand was neatly typed and from a man. It said,

Dear Ms. Hughes,

I understand what you were trying to say in your article about sexual fantasies, but I'm not so sure men can't be the way a woman imagines them. Take me, for example. I like to think I'm all the things you saw in Sam. I might not be quite as good-looking as him, but every woman I've gone out with says I'm sensitive *and* sexy.

You seem pretty tuned in to me and kind of lonely. Maybe the problem is you hav _n't met the right guy. I'm sure you've had lots of men writing and maybe you won't even read this, but I've had a fantasy of my own ever since I read your article. I see myself writing to ask you to have a drink with me after work, and you accepting.

How does the idea grab you? My name and number are at the bottom of this letter. Just so you know a little about me, I'm twenty-eight, five-ten, a hundred and eighty pounds. I ski and like moonlight walks on the beach....

Darien sighed and tossed the letter aside. There would be ten or twenty others just like it in the box, she was sure. But it didn't make her feel particularly good. Obviously some people weren't content with fantasies, they wanted to act on them. For the first time, she wondered if she'd created a monster.

Alan Maybank had called her the night before. He'd already dated her and been more or less rejected, but her article seemed to have rekindled his enthusiasm.

"You hide your passions well," he'd said. "I knew you were intelligent and attractive, but I didn't know you had all that fire inside."

"Only in my fantasies, Alan," she'd told him. "In real life I spend most evenings reading *Reader's Digest*."

He had laughed, but began catching on that the discovery of her simmering sexuality didn't change things between them. There had been no chance of her wanting to go to bed with him before she'd written the article, and there definitely wasn't now.

Virginia came in with another handful of phone messages and put the slips on the desk. Darien looked at her woefully.

"There's probably no point in writing them down," she said. "I'm not going to return any of these calls."

Virginia nodded. "Fine with me. I can keep a tally sheet and give it to you at the end of the day. I'm doing it for Mr. Smits anyway."

"Thanks." She sighed. "I don't suppose I've had any legitimate phone calls—from real people, I mean?"

The receptionist gave her a broad grin. Virginia was thirty-five, bone thin with frizzy blond hair. "Sometimes it's hard to tell. You wouldn't believe how sneaky some guys are. One insisted he was your older brother. I told him you didn't have one and he said he was a long-lost brother you didn't know about."

"Oh, Lord."

"There's lots of nut cases out there."

"I'm beginning to discover that. The next thing you know I'll be needing a bodyguard."

"The price of fame," Virginia said, cracking her gum. "Maybe you should go on the road. You could be the warm-up act for Madonna."

"Yeah, sure. I could read erotic poems or something. Maybe even try to ad-lib a fantasy about someone in the audience."

The receptionist chuckled. "Gotta look at the bright side. You never know when you'll run into a winner. At least, that's what my mother always told me. Well, I got to get back to my phones. Thank God, that's been more interesting the last couple of days. One guy calling for you even asked me out. Isn't that a hoot?"

"You should have accepted. He might be the love of your life, Virginia."

"Yeah, and if so I'll name my first kid after you."

They exchanged smiles and Virginia left. Darien turned to her computer as a telephone rang and rang somewhere across the newsroom. She switched on her monitor and stared at the blank screen.

Bob had told her to play around with some ideas for a follow-up article, and maybe even a series, but nothing had come to her yet.

But now, seeing the response her first piece had gotten, she wasn't so eager to plunge ahead. On the other hand, it was her job to write articles that sold newspapers. Her first editor at the *Post* claimed the secret of feature writing was to give readers what they wanted while always managing to surprise them. In this case, providing the surprise would be the difficult part.

Her fear was that she might be a one-note Johnny—able to come up with one whiz-bang article but incapable of sustaining her success. Darien told herself she simply had to get that kind of negative thinking out of her head. She was talented. She could do it. Unfortunately, though, her recent success had only served to make the pressure worse. Now there were even higher expectations.

Knowing a blank screen was the most daunting thing a writer could face, Darien began typing out random thoughts, just to get something down. She'd written a paragraph when she heard a light tap behind her. She turned around, expecting it to be another staffer, someone else come to razz her a little, but she couldn't have been more shocked.

He was in business attire, a light brown double-breasted European-cut suit with a dark brown Italian silk tie. He wore the same tinted glasses, gold cuff links, gold watch. The bemused smile was new, but he was no less handsome. Up close like this, he was almost breathtaking to look at.

"Hi," he said, "you're Darien Hughes, aren't you?"

Her mouth was hanging open. She only barely managed to nod.

"Can I assume, based on your reaction, that I might be Sam?"

Again she nodded, totally unprepared for what was happening. "How did—" she stammered, "uh . . . how—"

"Did I get in here?"

She nodded once more.

He removed his glasses and slipped them into his pocket. His eyes were a deep blue, as dark as hers were pale. They were gorgeous. "I've found that if you act like you belong someplace, people usually accept the fact that you do." He grinned.

It was a lovely, heart-wrenching smile. The man was more than handsome, he was beautiful. He had perfect cheekbones and evenly sculpted features. Yet he wasn't so good-looking that he was feminine. To the contrary he was very masculine—at least he struck her that way. She looked at him, only now beginning to get control of her senses.

"I—I never expected to see you again," she stammered.

"Actually I tried calling earlier," he said, "but judging by the receptionist's reaction, I decided you'd been getting lots of phone calls. I figured my chances of getting through weren't very good."

"Yes, my article seems to have caused a stir." She gripped the arms of her chair, thinking she ought to stand, but somehow she couldn't.

"It was quite good, by the way," he said. "I'm certainly no authority on journalism, but I found it . . . engaging."

Darien blushed, realizing she was face to face with the man she'd waxed so rhapsodic over, having undressed him and herself both in front of the entire San Francisco Bay Area. It hadn't been difficult to face him on paper, but this was different.

"I hope it isn't rude to drop in on you like this," he said, his speech as smooth and charming as his manner, "but I couldn't resist finding out if I was the Sam you wrote about and . . . well, frankly, seeing what sort of woman reacted to me that way."

"It wasn't you I was reacting to, Mr. . . . uh, Mr. . . . ?"

He shrugged. "Sam. Why destroy the illusion?"

Darien did not laugh when he chuckled. Instead she gave him a look, as if to say he was having a bit too much fun with this. His amusement was, after all, at her expense.

"I presume Sam is okay with you. After all, you named me," he said good-naturedly.

"Sure, Sam is fine. But let's be clear. You did inspire the piece, but the article wasn't about *you*, because I don't know you."

"Oh, I understand. Fantasy has nothing to do with reality, except to the extent it borrows bodies—in this case mine. I'm under no illusions, believe me."

"Then you came out of curiosity, and that's all?

"You wrote a provocative article and I felt a special . . . I don't know how to put it . . . let's say involvement in it."

Her cheeks colored. "I should have changed things around in the piece so you wouldn't have known. But as a reporter I have a habit of telling my stories straight. It didn't seem to matter because nobody knew who I was describing."

"Except for me, of course."

"Yes, I guess I discounted that."

"So we share a secret—just the two of us."

"That's not exactly true. A friend was with me that day. In a way, the idea was hers as much as mine."

He rubbed his chin. "You aren't sorry you wrote the article, are you?"

Darien looked at her hands. "No, I don't regret writing it, but I am embarrassed to be talking to you like this, if you want to know the truth. I certainly hadn't planned on seeing you again."

"I don't mean to embarrass you. Like I said, I was just curious, and that's why I came by."

"Well, I hope your curiosity's been satisfied, *Sam*."

The corners of his mouth curled. He studied her, looking her over without being obvious about it. He'd gone to some trouble to meet her, and evidently felt he ought to get his money's worth. "It has and it hasn't."

"Meaning?"

"I'm tempted to suggest we have lunch, but I can see it's probably a bad idea. You'd misunderstand my motives."

"You're probably right."

"There isn't an easy way of assuring you of my good intentions, is there?"

"What good intentions could you have? All I could possibly be to you is the woman who wrote that article. In every way but one, you're no different from the dozens of readers who felt compelled to write me or call and leave a message," she said, gesturing toward the box full of mail.

He smiled, showing his white teeth. "That's the problem, isn't it? You've put this scarlet S on my forehead and there's no easy way to get it off."

"You're right, Sam, lunch would only break the illusion. I intended that you would exist only in my fantasies, and it's best left that way."

"You seem very sure about that."

"And you seem to think the illusion is not enough," she said.

"In fairness, the fantasy was yours, not mine."

"I wrote a candid article about sexual fantasies. True, nobody talks about them much in polite company, but the truth is everyone fantasizes, all the time. Just because I had the guts to be up-front about it doesn't mean I wanted to set myself up as the target for everybody's lust." The indignation in her voice had risen to the point of anger.

"I don't recall suggesting we have sex, Ms. Hughes," he said calmly. "I believe what I suggested was lunch. I can see I was wrong to have come like this. I apologize for upsetting you. Please forgive me."

"No need to apologize. No harm's been done. We can return to our anonymity as if nothing ever happened."

"I don't see why we have to erase everything," he said. "I got vicarious pleasure out of your article, like everybody else. I'm flattered to have been the object of your fantasies." He gave her an utterly sincere look, his deep blue eyes exuding total innocence. "I hope by coming here I didn't destroy the illusion."

"No. Don't worry about it."

"Good." He stepped into the cubicle, extending his hand as a kind of peace offering.

Darien took it, aware of the strength in his long, thin fingers. His hand was much warmer than hers. She could almost feel the energy radiating from his fingers to hers. Then, when he gently started to pull his hand away, she realized he was about to leave without having revealed who he was.

Of course, considering the way she'd acted, she could hardly be surprised by that. Besides, a part of her was eager to be rid of him and the embarrassment. Yet another part of her regretted that their meeting was ending this way.

"Goodbye, Darien," he said. "Thanks for indulging me." He winked, turned and walked toward the elevators.

She listened to his receding footsteps until they were lost in the background sounds of the office—phones ringing, voices, the clatter of a printer. He was gone. It was suddenly over, as quickly and as unexpectedly as it had begun.

Was she missing an opportunity by letting him get away? Through the muddle in her brain she heard Maryanne's voice. "Don't let him leave, idiot! That's your fantasy come to life!"

Darien got to her feet and peered over the partition of her cubicle, looking in the direction he'd gone. She spotted him just as he disappeared out the exit at the far side of the newsroom.

She ran after him, nearly colliding with a messenger pushing a cart down the aisle. She arrived in the elevator lobby just as the doors closed. She was too late. He was gone. For good. She stood there numbly, telling herself it was just as well. But she wasn't so sure she believed it. The real Sam was every bit as exciting as the imaginary one. He was a charmer, just as she'd imagined. Probably a womanizer from the word go. And yet he was imminently likable. Simply put, she'd been intrigued.

The elevator doors suddenly opened, and there stood Sam, reincarnated before her very eyes. He looked as surprised as she.

"Going down?" he said.

Without thinking she stepped into the elevator. She looked at him from the corner of her eye.

"It was going up when I got on," he explained as the doors closed. "I didn't realize it until too late."

"Yes, it happens to me all the time."

A moment of silence passed.

"Are you headed out for lunch?" he asked.

"No, I'm, uh, going up to the corner for a bottle of aspirin." It was the only plausible explanation that came to mind.

"That's as good a commentary on your day as any, I suppose."

Darien nodded as the car came to a stop. The doors opened at the ground floor. Maryanne's voice screamed at her again. "Say something! This is your chance, Darien! Don't blow it!"

They stepped into the lobby. He walked silently beside her. One of Darien's favorite copy editors, a woman named Ellen, walked by, saying hello. She glanced at Sam and smiled before hurrying on. As they neared the main door, Darien stopped.

"Sam . . ."

He stopped, too, facing her. "Yes?"

"I'm thinking of doing another article about, uh, you, and I was wondering if . . . that is, I'm hoping you won't be . . ."

"Be what?"

"Offended or upset."

He chuckled, evidently finding the question amusing. "No, of course not. Anonymous celebrity is the best kind—not that it's really me you write about, because, as you correctly point out, you don't know me."

"True. But having spoken with you makes it different somehow. I didn't want to be presumptuous. Mentioning my intentions seemed only polite."

"Thank you," he said, "I appreciate your consideration."

They went to the door. He held it for her and they stepped onto the sidewalk, crowded with people headed for an early lunch. Her brain was spinning, part of her wanting to get the hell out of there as fast as she could, the other half desperately wanting to continue the conversation.

"Which way are you headed?" he asked.

She turned toward the shop on the corner where she had, in fact, bought a bottle of aspirin only the week before. "This way." The balmy wind blew her dark hair across her face, and she tucked it behind her ear. Sam discreetly glanced at her body.

"Me, too," he said.

They strolled along, Darien agonizing over what she was doing, feeling foolish, insane and desperate all at once. They were walking slowly. Darien sensed he was as reluctant to say a final farewell as she. It was within her power to break the impasse, but she couldn't bring herself to act. After all, this guy was a complete stranger—regardless of how intimate they'd been in her fantasies.

"Listen," he said, suddenly sounding very serious, "God knows, I don't want to interfere in any way, and you've made it clear you have no interest in me personally, but I am wondering if there might be a way I could help you with your work."

She looked at him, not sure what he was getting at.

"Let me put it this way," he went on. "You and I have sort of been playing a game. On the deck at Sam's, I was oblivious to what you were doing. Now I'm a participant. You still don't know me. As far as you're concerned, I'm Sam, the guy you invented. Maybe there's more about Sam to be learned, complexities you haven't imagined."

"I'm not sure I understand."

"That fellow you saw last Saturday inspired you once. He might again. For what it's worth, he's dining alone tonight at Perry's on Union Street, at eight o'clock. Observing him up close might give you some fresh insights."

They'd come to the corner and stopped in front of the shop. She looked into his eyes, searching for hidden motives, the danger she knew had to be there.

"I'm not trying to tell you your business," he said. "You're the writer. But if you want to do some further research into your subject, you'll know where to find me."

"You're being very clever," she said.

"Hey, you started this game. I was an innocent by-stander."

"You aren't so innocent now."

He shrugged. "I guess I've been hooked, Darien." He gave her a treacherously seductive smile. "Sam enjoys a good game. And there aren't many you can play where the rules are made up as you go along. That takes real creativity."

She gave him a wary look and his smile broadened. Again he extended his hand.

"It's been a pleasure," he said. "Maybe I'll see you around. But even if I don't, I'll be reading your articles with interest."

He turned and, seeing the traffic light about to change, dashed across the street. Once on the other side he continued up the sidewalk without looking back. She kept her eye on him until he disappeared into the lunchtime crowds. Sam knew damned well he'd piqued her interest. She'd bet her life on that. He was a bastard, she decided—a seductive one, but a bastard all the same.

3

"I DON'T SEE why you're so upset about meeting him," Maryanne said. "He sounds utterly charming to me. I'd go to Perry's. I'd have dinner with him. And I'd let him pay for it."

"Yeah," Darien said sardonically, "if I take the risk of meeting a total stranger, I ought to get a free dinner out of it, at least."

They were in Maryanne's office. Darien had called to see if she could drop by on her way home from work. Sitting in the big leather client chair, she almost felt as though it was a therapy session, not a conversation with a friend.

"I mean, really, what can happen?" Maryanne said. "Perry's is hardly a den of iniquity. And Sam doesn't sound like the type who's in the white slave trade."

"But I feel like I'm being manipulated. When I made it clear I wasn't interested in seeing him socially, he suggested that meeting him again might help me write another article."

"So call his bluff and do some research. Wasn't that how he phrased it?"

"Research, that's a joke. What could I possibly do with him that would constitute research? The whole point of a fantasy is that it's yours and yours alone."

"Oh? You'd be surprised how many people have sat in that chair, talking about wanting to act out their fantasies. Just because a dream starts out being private and

The place was in the rear garden of a Victorian. The property was owned by the man who ran the nursery where Janet Smits, an avid gardener, bought most of her statuary and plants.

According to Janet, Dean Wilson and his partner, Marc Boudre, had turned the two-story Victorian into flats, keeping the downstairs for themselves. The upstairs flat was rented to a woman obstetrician-gynecologist who spent most of her time at the hospital. But the one-bedroom mother-in-law cottage in the rear of the long narrow backyard was unoccupied. They would rent it for below market . . . but only to the right person.

Janet had warned her that both Dean and Marc were super picky about tenants. They were almost retired, artistic and very neat. As a couple, they had been together for years. The house was their dream home, and they wanted a tenant who wouldn't wreck the place with wild parties. As it turned out, Darien had liked Dean and Marc right from the first. And they'd taken her under their wing, treating her almost like a daughter.

She had go through a gate at the side yard and walk through a simply gorgeous rose garden to get to her cottage. Dean was nearly always doing something to improve the grounds, and Marc, a window dresser for a major downtown department store, was equally meticulous about the interior of the place. He was also a gourmet cook.

Darien opened the gate of the white picket fence and headed down the path. As she got past the main house, she saw that Dean was on his knees in the center of the yard, fussing with one of the rosebushes.

He always looked out of place to her when he worked in the garden, mainly because he was so very patrician looking—tall and slender with silver hair. But Dean never hesitated to get his hands dirty. He loved nurturing.

He looked up and grinned when she approached.

"Hey, Darien, come on over here and look at these Queen Mother roses. Have you ever seen anything so gorgeous? I think they're even better than the Sterling Silvers this year."

She walked over to him and dutifully sniffed a bud. Dean watched her.

"They're beautiful, Dean. Really lovely."

He regarded her carefully, his usual smile slowly dissolving. "Then why the long face, honey?"

She sighed. "It shows?"

He nodded.

"Well, to tell you the truth, I'm trying to decide what to do about a man."

Dean set down his shears and stood. A basket of cut roses in pinks, whites, lavenders and reds was at his feet. "Anything Marc or I can do?"

She shook her head. But then she thought better of it. "Not unless you're handing out free advice."

He chuckled. "Well, it will probably be worth what you pay for it, but I'll listen. We both will. Why don't you come on in with me and we'll have a glass of wine? Marc is making some sort of Greek dish tonight and he banished me from the kitchen. But for you, he'll make an exception."

He gathered the roses and ushered her into the house. The back door of the Victorian led to a mudroom that Dean had made into a potting area for his beloved plants. He opened a cupboard and took out a crystal rose bowl, then carefully put the flowers in it and filled the vase with water. He left it on the shelf by the sink.

"Don't you want to take them in?" Darien asked.

"No. I was cutting them for you. Marc and I were going to take them over to you after dinner along with some of the baklava he's making. As a treat. Besides, we have roses on practically every table in the house. Marc said one more vase and it will look like we're holding a wake."

Darien chuckled and followed Dean into the huge kitchen. Marc was apparently just finishing up his cooking because he was washing his hands and the kitchen was already spotless. A huge tray of baklava was sitting next to the sink. And she detected the odor of lemon and oregano and lamb coming from the oven. It smelled heavenly.

"Darien! Good to see you," Marc said. "Why didn't you show up earlier? I could have used some help."

"I would have given you a hand if you hadn't kicked me out," Dean said.

Marc put his hands on his hips. He was as short and stout as Dean was tall and slender. Like so many good cooks, he'd put on excess pounds sampling his own goodies. "Honestly. I needed a couple of extra hands, not ten green thumbs. Stick to the yard and I'll take care of the house." He turned to her. "How about a glass of wine? And I have a lovely triple cream cheese that is to die for. You can sit back and relax and we'll have a nice chat."

Darien laughed. "How about if I say yes to the wine, no to the cheese and yes to the chat? I can't eat anything if I'm going out tonight . . . at least, I *think* I might go out tonight." She turned to Dean.

"Let me guess. That's the man problem?"

She nodded.

Marc raised his eyebrows but didn't comment. Instead he took a bottle of Chardonnay from the refrigerator and opened it. He poured three glasses and put them on a tray. "Come on, let's go on into the living room." He looked over his shoulder at his partner. "Make sure you don't track any dirt in on my rug."

Dean dutifully checked his feet, then followed them into the living room. The men had furnished the room with authentic Victorian antiques. There were rosewood tables, two with marble tops. Instead of an uncomfortable horsehair sofa, they had opted for a lovely fat pink and yellow couch in an English rose chintz. With all the flowers in the room—on the mantel and on tables—the place looked like a garden. The fragrance was heady.

Darien sat on the couch, and Marc sat next to her. Dean took the chair across from them. He took a sip of wine and then said flatly, "Darien has a problem, Marc. A *man* problem. And she wants our advice."

Marc's eyes lit up. "Do tell. I want to hear it all!"

"Well," she began, "you know that article I did on sexual fantasies, the one that came out a couple of days ago?"

Dean nodded. "It was your best yet, in my opinion."

"While I was at work today the guy I saw last Sunday, out on the deck at Sam's, showed up."

Dean set down his glass. He seemed transfixed. "Your fantasy man? You mean he came to the *Bulletin* and actually spoke to you?"

"Yep. And he wants me to meet him for dinner tonight at Perry's."

Marc sighed. "Oh, that's so romantic. What are you going to wear?" He snapped his fingers. "I've got it. How about that darling navy suit of yours. You'd need dark hose and navy heels, though. Dark legs are so in now. I did a simply smashing window last week. All the hose were in dark shades to match the skirts. Very sexy."

Dean gave Marc a withering look. "Can't you see that the problem isn't what she's going to wear? Darien is worried about whether she should even meet this guy in the first place."

"Well, pardon me for breathing," Marc said. "I was simply trying to help. Heaven knows, *you* wouldn't know fashionable from fondue. And anyway, what a woman wears to meet a man is always important. Isn't that so, Darien?"

"Of course it is," she said. "But Dean is right, too. I'm not sure I should even see the guy again. I mean, I don't know a single thing about him."

"Quite right," Dean began. "You can't be too careful these days."

"Honestly, Dean, how is a girl supposed to meet anyone if she doesn't make an effort?" Marc turned to Darien and put his arm around her shoulder. "You already know the worst thing that could happen, sweetie—that he's a filthy bastard out to use you. But what if he isn't like that? What if he's wonderful? Do you want to kick yourself the rest of your life just because you were too chicken to find out? You aren't going to find the man of your dreams in a catalogue."

"Oh, use your head, Marc," Dean interjected. "The man of her dreams isn't going to show up at the *Bulletin* offering to take her out to dinner without even showing her the courtesy of telling her his name."

Darien sighed. "This one sure did."

"You see, Dean," Marc replied, "he *is* a dreamboat!" He gave his partner an I-told-you-so look. "Well, *I* think it's romantic, no matter what you say. I mean, how often does a guy like that show up in real life? Never! Most men have absolutely no imagination, and this one at least showed some originality. Not like you, so damned practical that you reason everything to death."

Dean huffed. "You ought to be glad that someone around here is practical. This isn't the 1950s. Darien has to be careful."

"Phooey. What can happen at Perry's? He's not going to drug her and carry her off to a life of prostitution, for heaven's sake."

"That was Maryanne's take on the situation, too," Darien said.

"Well, Maryanne is a lovely person," Dean said. "God knows, I think the world of her, but she may not have thought this thing through." He took a big sip of wine, keeping the glass in his hand. "You are both kind of young and trusting, and when you're single looking for someone special, something like this has . . . a certain romantic appeal—"

"You got that right," Marc agreed.

Dean put down his glass so hard that Darien was afraid it would break. "Would you stop interrupting me, Marc? The point I'm trying to make is, if a guy needed a great lure, what would be better than tuning in to a woman's fantasy? This fellow sounds like he could be a manipulator. I'd think twice about going, Darien."

"For heaven's sake," Marc said, "the fellow suggested dinner, not a weekend in the country. If she takes a taxi, she can leave whenever she wants. For that matter, she can look over the situation when she gets there and leave if the set-up isn't to her liking. That ought to be safe enough, even for you."

"That's not such a bad idea," Darien said. She turned to Marc. "Thanks."

Marc looked smug. He took a sip of wine and mouthed an "I-told-you-so" in Dean's direction for a second time. Dean scowled.

Darien decided the time had come to leave. "I really appreciate the two of you helping me like this. Talking it over with you has helped clarify my thoughts." She turned to Marc and gave him a quick peck on the cheek. "I like your idea about the navy suit, too. *If* I go, that's what I'll wear. But I'll have a long soak in the tub and think over everything you guys have said before I decide for sure."

She stood. Marc and Dean got up, as well. As Darien made her way to the kitchen, Dean followed. Marc stayed behind to pick up the wineglasses.

When she got to the back door she reached up and patted Dean's cheek. "Thanks for the advice. It's nice to know you care."

He gave her arm a squeeze. "Anytime, honey." He stepped into the mudroom, got the vase of roses and handed it to her. "We'll come by later with the baklava. And to make sure you're okay."

"She'll be fine," Marc added, setting down the tray of glasses on the counter by the sink. "If you go, sweetie, don't forget the dark hose. They'll make your legs look fabulous."

She grinned. "I won't. And thanks to both of you."

DARIEN LEANED BACK in her old-fashioned bathtub, luxuriating in the warm bubbles. Her bathroom was quaint and feminine. Marc had decorated it with pink striped wallpaper that had a floral border at the ceiling. With the big old porcelain tub and the Victorian toilet with the water tank close to the ceiling and a pull-chain flush, the room looked like something out of the 1800s. She absolutely loved it.

In a way, the cottage was a fulfillment of a fantasy. Even before Dean had opened the front door that first time and she'd seen the hardwood floors, the fireplace with the marble mantel and the tiny perfect kitchen, she had known she wanted to live here in the middle of a rose garden. The place was like a dream come true.

That was funny, because she'd had that same kind of gut-level reaction to Sam. She'd known he was special, too, right from the start. It wasn't only that he was handsome, there was something about the way he held himself, and the way he reacted to others, that called to her.

She'd told Maryanne at the restaurant that Sam had struck her as a predator. But now that she'd seen him up close and talked to him she knew that wasn't quite right. The only problem was, she wasn't sure how she'd characterize him. Maybe Dean had a point—maybe she was so needy to have someone truly special in her life that she'd sold herself a bill of goods.

She sighed. She had thought she was well beyond that, but perhaps she wasn't. In any case, if she went to Perry's, as she was now inclined to do, she would no doubt know a lot more about Sam before the evening was over. In fact, she fully expected to be thoroughly disillusioned in a matter of a few hours. That was such a shame. Darling cottages in rose gardens might be hard to find, but they did exist. But if she'd learned anything in her thirty years, it was that fantasy lovers did not come to life. They couldn't, because reality never quite lived up to a dream.

Darien reached out with her foot and turned the tap to put more hot water into the tub. When she had it the way she wanted, she scrunched down until the water lapped at the back of her neck where she'd pinned up her hair, and closed her eyes. At least now, at this very moment, Sam was still perfect. Gorgeous, charming. It was so easy to build a fantasy around him.

His voice was rich and deep. Before he had shown up at the *Bulletin* she hadn't known what color his eyes were, nor had she had a good look at his hands. Darien sighed as she wondered what it would feel like if those long fingers of his were touching her now. What if Sam walked into this room and found her? Would he strip and get in the bathtub with her? Would he play at washing her back as an excuse to caress her, or would he boldly put his hands on her breasts? Or would Sam simply scoop her out of the water and carry her into the bedroom where he'd make wild, passionate love to her?

Dear God, any of them sounded good. Terrific, actually. In all her years of dating she could honestly say she'd never met a man who was the masterful, sweep-you-right-off-your-feet type. Of course, even if she had met someone like that, she probably wouldn't have liked him—not in real life.

She'd given up her virginity to her first serious boyfriend in college. Even at the time, Darien had known she wasn't truly in love, not the way she wanted to be. Then, when she met Todd, she had been in love and it was wonderful.

They'd met at a wedding held in the chapel at Amherst. Darien was a bridesmaid for one of her sorority sisters, and Todd had been the groom's cousin. They had hit it off right from the first, discovering a mutual love for old mystery movies. That summer they went to every film Alfred Hitchcock had ever made, at least twice. Which was just as well because they'd both been far more interested in each other than they had been in seeing the movies.

Todd had a sister who was nearly ten years older than he was, and for him that had been almost like being an only child. Since his parents, like hers, were older when he was born, he understood what Darien meant when she said she felt alien from her family. But once she and Todd found each other, none of that mattered. Neither of them would ever be lonely again.

Then Todd had been killed in that boating accident. Darien had gone to New York with her mother to shop for a wedding dress that day. When they got back to their hotel room there was a message to call home. Her father gave her the grim news. As long as she lived she'd never forget the pang of emptiness she felt deep in her soul when she learned that Todd was dead.

The water suddenly felt cold. Darien pulled the plug and stood up. She reached for a towel and stepped onto the bath mat. A film of bubbles coated her skin. As she began drying herself she realized it had been a long time since she'd thought about that terrible day. Years.

Her goals now were different. She didn't think about marriage or sharing her life with one perfect man. Dreams like that were too easily destroyed. It was a hell of a lot better to fantasize about someone like Sam who was sexy but safe . . . so long as he remained a fantasy lover.

But maybe that was the point. Bob Smits had challenged her to delve a little deeper into her feelings, to get in touch with herself. Maryanne and Marc had said much the same thing, though their styles had been different. Even Dean, the voice of caution and reason, had allowed that she'd be safe if she used her head. Well, she thought as she hung up her towel and unpinned her hair, she was going to go for it.

Half an hour later Darien had touched up her hair and makeup and had dressed. As she put on the fake pearl earrings that looked so good with her navy suit, she checked the clock on the mantel in the main room. It was a few minutes to eight. The taxi would be out front soon.

Darien regarded her image in the antique Venetian mirror she'd bought with some of the money her grandmother had left her. She looked good. A little nervous, but good. Her dark hair was thick and shiny and for once it had cooperated, smoothly curving under on both sides. Marc had been right about the suit. Worn without a blouse, it split the difference between being professional and sexy.

She grabbed her small navy bag and went out the front door, carefully locking it behind her. As she walked through the rose garden, she realized how lucky she was to have Dean and Marc for landlords. They truly cared about her. That was a blessing.

In fact, now that she thought about it, she was fortunate, indeed. She'd made good friends since coming to San Francisco. Her job was a fantastic opportunity, and her writing was getting better all the time. And, thanks to her latest article, she had a once-in-a-lifetime chance to live out a fantasy. What more could a woman possibly ask for?

She stepped through the gate to the pathway leading to the sidewalk. As she shut it, she looked at the main house. Dean and Marc were standing in the window of the living room, watching her.

The taxi arrived a moment later and Darien got in. As they pulled away from the curb, she turned to take a final look at the old Victorian. Dean and Marc were both waving to her, wishing her luck. That made her feel good because she was certain she was going to need it.

4

DARIEN nervously fumbled through her purse to get the right amount of money to pay the taxi driver. Then she got out of the cab and looked across the street at Perry's familiar red awning.

Her first week on the *Bulletin,* Bob Smits had taken her and three other reporters to lunch there. Rod Barker had been one. He'd been newly hired, as well, having recently arrived from L.A. But being a native Californian, he'd spent a lot of time in San Francisco and he knew the city. Rod had told her that Perry's was popular with writers. Three nationally syndicated columnists who wrote for the *Chronicle* called the watering hole their home away from home.

Darien walked down the brick alleyway to the side entrance. A long mahogany bar ran half the length of the room, which was packed, as usual. There were a few tables in the very front of the restaurant, facing Union Street, but she hadn't spotted Sam at any of them. He was either in back, which was the main dining room, or he hadn't shown up.

She tapped her foot, trying to sort out her options. First she would check out the back room. If Sam was there, she could decide whether to join him or cut her losses and head home. If he wasn't there yet, or if he didn't show up at all, then the decision would be made for her. She'd have to content herself with writing a fabulous article on the experience—"What it's like to be stood up by a fantasy man!" At least that way she could put her taxi bill on her expense report to the *Bulletin.*

Darien made her way past the throng at the bar, getting more than one interested look from the men gathered there. She headed down the narrow hallway, past the photos of sports and political figures, to the rear dining room. The game she'd played as a little girl when she'd pulled petals off a daisy ran through her brain. Sam would be there; Sam wouldn't be there; he would; he wouldn't. She was on the third "he wouldn't" when she spotted him. He was sitting alone at a table for two in the back corner. The mahogany-paneled wall behind him was partly covered by a huge chalkboard that listed the day's specials.

She let out a long, slow breath as she silently watched him, trying to decide whether to proceed. He was oblivious to her, writing something in a little notebook of some sort. His head was bowed, but there was a simple elegance in that gesture that she found appealing. His every move as he wrote was graceful. Sam put down his pen and slipped the notebook in his pocket. As he did, he glanced up and spotted her. He got to his feet, smiling.

"I'm delighted you've come," he said as she approached the table. "I wasn't sure you would."

"I wasn't so sure myself."

"Oh?"

He pulled out a chair and helped her into her seat. Then he cleared his throat in a self-conscious sort of way, smiled again and sat down. Now that she was closer to him, Darien could see that he was nervous, too. He'd acted completely in control that morning. But now he seemed endearingly human. This chink in his armor made him even more desirable.

"Even on my way over in the taxi I was having second and third thoughts," she said.

"What made you finally decide?"

"I'm not sure."

He nodded, as if he understood perfectly. "I figured the odds were fifty-fifty."

Darien chuckled. "You weren't sure which was greater—my curiosity or good judgment. Is that it?"

"I'd rather think it was curiosity *and* good judgment."

She took her napkin and spread it on her lap. "I suppose we'll see, Sam, won't we?"

"I have a hunch we aren't the only ones waiting to see what happens next. The entire Bay Area is eager to read your next article. Frankly, I'm curious about it myself."

"Is that a subtle way of saying you're serious about helping with my work—that inviting me here wasn't just a ploy?"

"No, it wasn't a ploy. I'm taking your work very seriously."

Darien gave him a long penetrating look as she evaluated his words. Did he truly mean what he said or was he playing with her? But what worried her most was that she couldn't read the man very well. Did that mean he was an accomplished liar, a con? Or was it that she'd met her match? Not knowing made her uneasy. "Then tell me, why am I so suspicious?"

"Maybe it has more to do with you than with me."

Their eyes locked. He seemed bemused, but she could tell he was struggling not to let it show. She couldn't help wondering if he *had* sensed something in her. Was Sam one of those men with infallible instincts about women, one who could read them like an open book? She'd never known anyone like that, but she'd heard about them—men with an uncanny knowledge of the female psyche.

"Am I wrong?" he asked when she didn't say anything.

"Maybe you're right," she said. "But the suspicion I feel is real enough, believe me."

"Fear of the unknown, perhaps."

"You may be right about that," she said. "As a fantasy man you were safe. But now, face to face, there are other issues."

"What can I do to put you at ease?" he asked.

The tiny smile that followed gave her pause. She searched Sam's face for signs of sincerity. It was there, all right, but she was afraid to trust it. She took a deep breath, watching him carefully. Her wariness elicited a gentle smile from him, but it wasn't enough to make her let down her guard.

As she continued to gaze into his eyes, she was still trying to decide whether his smoothness necessarily meant he was false. Could this seeming naturalness of his be real? And who was Sam, anyway? she asked herself. An actor? A gigolo?

"If your eyes tell the story, I'm in trouble," he said.

"My skepticism is that obvious, is it?"

He nodded.

"Forgive me, but this is not an everyday thing with me. The real me—the woman and writer—lives in the world of work and deadlines and paying bills and getting on with her life. And the other me—the one who occasionally indulges in fantasies—well, she prefers the world of make-believe. In every way that counts, she and I exist in two different realms."

"And now you find those two worlds colliding. You don't have to explain, Darien. I really do understand that," he said. "And I'm here to help."

"Why?"

He thought for a moment. "I'm curious. And I find you intriguing. Is that a sufficiently evasive answer?"

"At least you're consistent," she said with a laugh. "I guess that's good."

"I aim to please."

She arched a brow. "Good. Then in the interest of friendly relations I want to make one thing very clear," she said. "I'm here as a writer, not as a woman who sometimes likes to indulge in fantasies." She paused to let the words sink in.

"You're saying you're having dinner with me for the sake of your readers, not for your own sake."

"Yes, that's as good a way to put it as any. I hope that's all right with you."

"Certainly, but my motives may be a bit more selfish," he said.

His seeming candor gave her pause. He apparently saw the look of uncertainty on her face, because he went on.

"It *is* all right if I enjoy myself, isn't it?" he asked.

"I can't help wondering if I shouldn't be asking more questions," she said.

"Surely Sam has his secrets."

"You're asking me?"

"He is your creation, isn't he?"

"The Sam I wrote about, yes. But are we talking about him, or are we talking about you?" she asked.

"Oh, I think him. As you said, you're here as a writer. So I presume it's Sam you came to have dinner with. In any case, it seems we are going to have the good fortune to collaborate a bit. That's something to celebrate."

With incredibly good timing, the waiter arrived just then with a bottle of French champagne and two flutes. Darien's eyes widened when she saw the label. Either Sam had money to throw around or he was putting on a show. She recalled the way he'd been dressed when she'd first seen him—the white linen shirt that had probably set him back a couple of hundred dollars, the gold watch. And the suit he wore today looked like it had cost a bundle, too.

Sam had money and he wasn't afraid to spend it. Those were two things she now knew about him. But that made her wonder all the more about the things she didn't know—like who he really was and what he did for a living. She couldn't very well ask, not until they'd come to an understanding.

"I hope you don't mind," he said, interrupting her thoughts, "but I took the liberty of ordering some wine, just in case we decided to proceed."

"Interesting way to put it," she observed.

"When you come right down to it, our relationship is somewhat awkward, isn't it? We'll get that straightened out, though." He winked.

She watched silently as the waiter poured champagne into two flutes. Then he put the open bottle in an ice bucket next to the table and withdrew. Sam picked up his glass, and she did, as well.

"How about if we drink to your fantasies?" he said in his silky deep voice. "After all, without them we wouldn't be here."

Darien touched her glass to the one he'd extended across the table. When she looked into his incredible dark blue eyes, her breath wedged in her throat. She actually had to remind herself to breathe again before taking a sip of the champagne and putting her flute down.

"It seems to me the first order of business is to figure out what you want to write about," he said. "Everything else we do or say depends on it."

"That makes sense. Do you have a suggestion?"

"You spoke earlier of existing in two different realms—the real world and the world of fantasy. Tonight they've come together. Why not write about that?"

"You mean I should compare the Sam in my fantasies with the flesh and blood person?"

"Well, that's one approach, I suppose. Another might be to act your fantasies out. See how they play in real life. In me, Darien, you have a willing, able and understanding collaborator."

She chuckled and sipped her champagne. "Isn't that a rather self-serving suggestion, Sam? Or am I just being paranoid?"

He turned the stem of his glass between his fingers. "What does it matter, so long as you get what you want? Journalistically speaking, of course."

"Let's be a little more specific," she said. "What, exactly, are you proposing?"

"Simply put, let's continue the game. The first round was in your head. Now you're having dinner with Sam, face to face. I'm sort of like the statue that's come to life."

"Yes, but you aren't Sam, at least you're not *my* Sam," she protested.

"Oh, but I am."

"How could you be?"

He reached inside his coat pocket and removed a newspaper clipping. Unfolding it, he began to read.

"I believe the most miraculous thing of all was how well Sam understood me. He seemed to anticipate my every thought, my every desire, yet at the same time he managed to surprise me. He was good-looking, yes, he was intelligent, well-mannered, charming, amusing, yes, yes, yes, yes, yes. But all those things paled beside the profound connection I felt with him.

"In an odd way, Sam seemed to know me better than I knew myself. He knew what I wanted before I did. He understood that my need to be loved was only the beginning. My body needed to be fed, but so did my soul and my imagination. He understood that danger and mystery were as important as tenderness and affection. Sam knew that my strengths needed challenging just as my weaknesses needed nurturing. Quite simply, Sam knew what it was to be me."

Sam carefully folded the clipping and returned it to his pocket. Then he clasped his hands and looked at her. Darien felt her heart rocking. The longer the silence endured, the harder it seemed to beat.

"Those are my words," she said, barely managing a whisper.

"But they describe me."

"Anybody could say that," she protested. "Dozens of men tried. They called. They wrote letters...."

"But I was the one you saw."

He drank some wine, looking at her over the rim of the glass. His endearing, not-so-innocent smile said, "Trust me." But she didn't. And yet, at the same time, she could tell he truly had understood the words she'd written, whether in fact they were descriptive of him or not.

"You're very clever, Sam," she said.

"I believe you expect that of me."

"Maybe too clever."

"I sincerely hope not."

"You must have something specific in mind," she said, sipping her wine.

"I think you should put yourself in my hands. That's what you want to do in your heart of hearts."

Darien laughed nervously.

"I'm serious," he said.

"I'm sure you are!"

"What do you find objectionable?"

"What kind of fool do you take me to be? Suggesting I put myself in your hands is the most blatantly self-serving thing you've said yet."

"What are you afraid of?" he asked.

"I don't know you from Adam. And Russian roulette is not my idea of creative journalism. I might as well walk into the bar and pick up the first good-looking guy I see!"

"Ah, but you *do* know me, Darien. You don't know yet how well, but you do. And that's the point of all this—to satisfy yourself that it's true. You see, life is a game. And this is a very specific game that you and I have the opportunity to play.

"You're a salesman, Sam," she said, picking up her glass. "And a very successful one, I'll bet. What do you sell? Commodities? Futures? Or just yourself?"

He grinned.

"You're having a good time," she said. "You probably have money riding on this—bets with your friends."

"No," he said, shaking his head, "I haven't discussed this with a soul. I took your article to heart, Darien. Like it or not, you really were describing me."

"And I'm supposed to take that on faith?"

"Of course not," he replied. "But we can't proceed until you know where I'm coming from. You asked a direct question, and I'm trying to answer it as candidly as possible."

"You're playing with me."

"Yes. I'm enjoying this, because I enjoy you. And deep down, you understand that. I don't profess to be perfect, but I am, or can be, the man you described."

"Those aren't quite the same."

"The ambiguity appeals to me. And if you're honest, Darien, you'll admit it appeals to you, too. You like the game as much as I do. Maybe better."

"You have a very big ego," she said.

"Are you saying Sam doesn't?"

Darien didn't respond because she knew he was right. She watched as he took the champagne bottle from the ice bucket and filled their glasses.

"Maybe we should define our terms," she said. "What does putting myself in your hands mean, exactly?"

"The simplest way to answer that is to allow me to be Sam. Then I'll show you."

"I can control my fantasies," she said. "But I have no reason to trust you."

"I understand that trust must be earned. I intend to make this as comfortable for you as I can because if you don't get pleasure out of it, then I'll have failed. And worse, you'd have nothing to write about—at least in a family newspaper," he added with another wink.

The waiter came to take their orders. Darien welcomed the excuse to look over the menu. She needed a respite, a chance to clear her thoughts. This guy was proposing to step right into her fantasies. And he made the prospect sound very appealing. She was actually tempted!

She skimmed the menu quickly while the waiter added a splash of champagne to her glass. She immediately picked it up and took a gulp, reading without really see-ing what they had to offer.

"Would you like more time?" Sam asked her.

"Well, no, I'm sure I can find something."

"Do you like seafood?" he asked.

"Yes."

"You might like the Dungeness crab, then."

"Okay. Sounds good."

"Two orders of crab," Sam said to the waiter.

"And would you care for something to start?" the man asked.

"Darien?" Sam said.

"Would you like to split a Caesar salad?" she asked.

"I was going to suggest it myself."

The waiter went away.

"Now where were we?" she asked.

Sam thought for a moment before answering. "Dar-ien, I propose that we proceed a step at a time, just as long as it feels comfortable. You'll always have the power to accept or reject.

"For example, I invited you to dinner. You came. I suggested crab, you accepted. But you could have or-dered differently, if you chose. The same will be true of dessert."

"And what does Sam have in mind for *after* dessert?"

He looked deep into her eyes. "I think a stroll along Union Street."

"And then?"

"Then I'll put you in a cab and send you home."

Darien smiled.

"Sam recognizes the value of subtlety," he said smoothly. "We have to keep your readers wondering. The expectation is half the fun."

"Expectation of what?"

"The next step."

"Which is?"

"Sam will let you know in due course. But might I suggest you keep your weekend open?" He fiddled with his flute, slowly turning it while staring at the pale liquid. "Quality fantasies require imagination and planning."

His words rolled off his tongue suggestively, sending a pulse through her. Darien found herself both mesmerized and intrigued. She watched him drink his wine and she sipped some of her own. God, he was smooth.

She hoped the little shudder that went through her wasn't noticeable. The last thing she wanted was for him to know he'd gotten to her. Sam—the one in her fantasies—had come to life before her eyes. He was plotting something for the weekend, expecting that she would willingly go along.

"What are you thinking?" she asked.

"I truly don't know yet," he said. "I'll have to give it some thought. But it must be worthy of Sam."

Worthy of Sam, she thought. Lord, could she live with that? Sam—her Sam, at least the one she'd created in her imagination—was capable of a hell of a lot that never made the paper.

"Is that color I see in your cheeks?" he asked.

Darien glanced at the nearest table to make sure no one was listening to them. Thankfully, the young couple seated there seemed totally absorbed in each other. She managed to look into Sam's eyes. "This game of yours might be a little dangerous for my blood," she said.

"We'll do only what pleases you, Darien. I can hardly be fairer than that."

"I wish I knew what you had in mind—not specifically, but generally."

"Use your imagination, Darien. I'll have to."

"Sam," she said, lowering her voice, "all kidding aside, don't you think this is getting a little kinky? I mean we're amusing ourselves and all, but underneath it's a little much, don't you agree?"

"Is that an oblique reference to sex?"

She glanced around the room again. No one was paying attention to them. "That is what I'm asking, I suppose."

"I've already said that whatever I propose you must approve."

She rolled her eyes. "That's what I was afraid you'd say."

"Leave it to me, Darien."

He was exactly the way Sam would be. That was so unnerving. This guy had her fantasy man down cold. What she wasn't sure was if that was a testimonial to him or to her writing ability.

"It's hard to let go, I know," he said, as though he'd been reading her thoughts. "The world is so full of disappointment. Believing is not easy. It takes courage to trust your heart."

"You've got Sam's silver tongue down pat," she said.

He smiled. "I hope you take that as a good sign."

"How did you know I'd fall for this? Was it the article?"

He shrugged. "The article. Seeing you. Observing you. A lot more passes between people than just words. You know what I mean. You felt it for Sam."

Darien shivered. "Lord," she said, "I don't believe this."

The waiter arrived with their salad, then left. They didn't speak. She looked at Sam long and hard. He didn't flinch. He didn't turn away or flush or speak. He simply sat there, as if he knew she needed time to assess him, to digest what had happened.

She took a deep breath. In thirty years she'd never once dreamed that she'd find herself in a situation like this. Yet if she was absolutely honest with herself, she'd have to admit that a part of her—a hell of a big part of her—liked it a whole lot. That, perhaps, was the most disconcerting thing of all. It was like Sam was giving her a fresh look at herself, revealing a part of her she hadn't been completely in tune with.

The words he'd read from her article rang in her ears. "The most miraculous thing of all was how well Sam understood me. He seemed to anticipate my every thought, my every desire, yet at the same time he managed to surprise me." Was she deluding herself? she wondered. Or was this real?

She took a few bites of salad, then drank some wine. Sam was content to let the silence hang. It was as though he knew she was making her decision. He'd made his case and now he was waiting—like a lawyer who'd finished his summation and knew the verdict was in the jury's hands.

Did she want to play his game? And if so, what did that mean? He'd invited her to act out her fantasies, and everyone knew fantasies were ultimately about sex. The irony was that rather than disgusting her, the notion aroused her. When she considered what it would be like to put herself in his hands—let him have his way with her—she began trembling.

Then, almost as though he'd been reading her thoughts, Sam reached for her hand and took it in both of his. She felt the smoothness of his palm. A warm energy flowed from his fingers to hers. His thumb absently rubbed the back of her hand. She gazed into his eyes—

those incredibly deep blue eyes—and told herself she just might be a goner.

"You worry too much," he said softly. "You need to relax."

When she pulled her hand from his she saw a tiny smile at the corner of his mouth. She wondered if it meant he understood just how successful and insightful he'd been. Probably.

Darien knew she could defy him. She could get up and walk out, or tell him the dinner was nice but to forget the weekend. She could do that if she wanted to. The problem was she didn't. She wanted exactly what was happening, and it was for the very reason she'd invented Sam in the first place. She was a woman in need and that was a truly frightening thing to discover.

"You've given me a lot to consider," she said, feeling she had to explain herself.

Sam sat there silently, waiting, watching her. He was too smart to press her.

The busboy cleared their salad plates. The waiter came, draining the last of the champagne into their glasses and asking if they wanted another bottle.

Sam looked at her. "It goes well with the crab," he said. "And neither of us is driving."

She shrugged. Sam signaled the waiter to bring another.

"You took a taxi, too?" she said.

"No, I have a driver."

Darien's brows rose.

"It's the best way to beat the parking problem," he explained.

"If I ever get around to buying a car, I'll keep that in mind."

"We seem to have a common appreciation for champagne," he said.

"Yes. As a matter of fact, I was drinking champagne the day I saw you on the deck at Sam's."

"Oh?"

"It was my birthday. My friend Maryanne bought it for me. Special occasion. I turned thirty."

He cocked his eyebrow. "I'd have guessed younger. But then, maybe not. Thirty is perfect. Old enough to have the courage to live out a fantasy." He gave her a penetrating look.

Darien's insides turn to mush. She swallowed hard and took a deep breath. "As regards the weekend, Sam, I'll listen to what you propose, but I won't make any promises."

He seemed pleased. "Good. Now I've got to come up with an offer you can't refuse." Then he gave her his wry smile, the one that had been bedeviling her all evening.

She sighed, hating herself for being weak, for letting him win. "I hope I'm not making a mistake," she ventured aloud.

"You aren't, Darien, I promise. And I'll promise you this, too—I'm going do everything in my power to make your fantasy everything you ever dreamed of." He paused dramatically. "And maybe everything you've been afraid to dream of, too."

5

As I lay sleepless in my bed that night I wondered if I'd been duped. Could Sam be an opportunist who knew an easy mark when he saw one? Was I too dumb, too naive or too blind to see what he was up to?

The romantic side of me resisted. I couldn't give up hope that my fantasy man was real and true and wonderful as I had made him out to be. I couldn't reject him out of hand. That would have been much too practical. I didn't want to be wise any more than I wanted to be right.

And yet I was a woman. Women easily became victims, if they allowed themselves to be used. So what did that mean? That I should reject him out of hand, just to be safe?

Then I thought maybe Sam the person wasn't so important as Sam the fantasy. Wasn't what was in my head the part that really mattered? Sam might have been the clay, but I had been the sculptress. His smile, his touch, his soft words were but trees falling in a silent forest if I hadn't been there to see and feel and hear them.

Oh, Sam was magical all right, but what is a magician without an audience? The magic is in the beholding, the imagining, the loving. A lover must have a partner to be a lover. Without me, Sam would have been an empty gesture. Alone, he was but a single hand clapping.

But if the magician needs the audience, the audience also needs the magician. I wanted the magic badly enough that I willingly put myself into Sam's hands. I had taken the game to the next level. I was ready for Wonderland. I trusted that Sam knew what to do, that he wouldn't let me down, that he understood my needs and desires as well as I. Maybe even better.

DARIEN SET ASIDE the article that had appeared in the *Bulletin* two days earlier and looked at her computer. She sighed. She'd been staring at a nearly blank screen for hours. She'd hoped that by rereading the article she'd written following their dinner at Perry's, inspiration would come to her. But she'd spent most of her time speculating on what Sam had thought when he'd read it.

It was Wednesday, five days had passed since their dinner, and she hadn't heard a peep from him. Maybe he'd had second thoughts about the game. Or maybe, after reading the article, he'd had second thoughts about her.

The second piece had been every bit as successful as the first. The initial mail and the phone calls had been positive and supportive. People—women readers in particular—were deriving vicarious pleasure from her experience, encouraging her. "Go for it!" "Grab the guy!" "Any extra hunks you can send my way?" were the comments she was getting.

The reaction at the paper was equally positive. She had gotten a warm note from Roger Gilbert, the publisher, saying she was doing a great job and to keep up the good work. That made her feel terrific, but it also upped the pressure. What if Sam fizzled out on her? What would she do then?

Even if she never saw Sam again, having dinner with him had been quite an experience. All weekend she'd been in a state of shock. Not that anything earthshaking had happened, but it was not a date she'd ever likely forget. She'd recorded it faithfully in her article, waxing rhapsodic about the champagne and crab, the sexual bantering and their wildly romantic dessert—especially the dessert. Even now, thinking about the way they'd shared an apple brown Betty made her insides go soft and mushy.

The waiter had brought two spoons but before Darien could pick up hers, Sam had offered her a bite from his. There was something awfully sexy about that. First he would take a bite, slowly putting the spoon in his mouth, his deep blue eyes on her as he turned the spoon over and licked every trace of the whipped cream off it. Then he'd offer her the next bite.

As he fed her, she watched the expression in his eyes. They seemed extra dark, almost passionate. Sam was making love to her with his eyes. It didn't take a genius to see that. She saw the challenge on his face when he offered her a bite of dessert, and the triumph when she licked the spoon as he had.

When his tongue darted out to moisten his lower lip, Darien had pictured him licking her flesh the way he had the whipped cream. She could almost feel the prickly bumps on his tongue as she imagined them being drawn up the side of her neck or over the tops of her breasts. And then, after the last bite, Sam had reached over with his fingertip and removed a trace of cream from the corner of her mouth. When he'd gazed deep into her eyes and licked that bit of cream off his finger afterward, Darien had felt a rush of liquid between her legs.

Sam had managed to convey a great deal with very few words and a number of gestures. She marveled at the fact that she'd practically been ready to go to bed with the man and he hadn't so much as kissed her! If ever there was proof of the power of fantasy, that was it.

She'd let herself play his exciting game, perhaps because that was the reason she'd gone in the first place— to get inspired. After all, Sam supposedly was the object of her research. But by the same token, she hadn't been in a hurry for the evening to end.

The problem was that the line between her personal and professional life was becoming blurred. Drawing on her passions, she'd let herself get sucked in a little too deep. Fortunately nothing had happened to cause her great embarrassment. But she'd known what effect Sam was having on her, and that was enough to put her on guard.

On Saturday she'd talked to Maryanne about her concerns. "In my opinion, it's a lot more significant that you're worrying about it than the fact that it happened," Maryanne had said. "I think you've got to relax a little. There's nothing that says your work can't be enjoyable."

"I all but agreed to spend the weekend with the man," Darien had said. "Don't you think that's going a bit further than just trying to enjoy my work?"

"That depends, kiddo. How many women can honestly say their work is writing about their sexual fantasies? Anyway, all that matters is that you're safe, and Sam seems to have recognized the importance of that."

Darien hadn't protested too strongly, mainly because she wasn't even sure the next step would come to pass. With each day, she'd wondered more and more if it would. Maybe her clever little gimmick had played itself out.

Ironically everybody at the *Bulletin*, not to mention a large segment of the greater Bay Area, also wondered what would happen next. About half an hour earlier Rod Barker had dropped by to suggest she have Sam take her to Candlestick Park so she could play out a fantasy in one of the sky boxes during a Giant's game. It was easy to see where his mind was. It also pointed out that lots of people were getting off on this thing—and worse still, that they seemed to want to share their fantasies in the process.

Virginia had volunteered that her sexiest fantasy involved being locked in a candy factory overnight with Mel Gibson. The way Virginia had it figured, they'd lick milk chocolate off each other all night. Darien had laughed, mainly because she wasn't sure which turned Virginia on more, the thought of Mel Gibson or being able to eat all the chocolate she wanted.

Even as she was thinking about Virginia, Darien heard her voice. She was three cubicles away, talking to Carolyn Buchanan, the reporter who wrote the weekly decorating column. From what Darien could gather, they were discussing how throw pillows in assorted pastels were a good and inexpensive way to brighten a bedroom. Virginia regularly schmoozed Susan Pfeiffer, too. Susan was the food editor, and whenever the receptionist wanted cooking tips she always went to Susan. Darien was beginning to see that she had become Virginia's consultant on sex.

Just then Virginia walked by. Darien stopped her.

"There hasn't been a message from Sam, has there?" she asked.

The thin blonde screwed up her face as she chewed her gum, popping it. She smelled of cinnamon. "Nope, not the real one, anyway. Two more phonies tried, but I'm getting so I can spot them without having to ask many questions."

Earlier Virginia had told her that whenever someone called saying he was Sam, she asked him what Darien Hughes looked like. That usually ended the discussion. But they'd agreed that if she and Sam continued to play the game, he would need a new name, known only to them, or a password.

"Well, I hope he calls soon," Darien said. "I'm working on a deadline."

"If it was me," Virginia said, "the deadline would be the last thing I'd be worried about. I could get used to dates with this Sam real fast."

Darien shrugged.

"Come on," Virginia said, "tell the truth. If you weren't writing for the paper, wouldn't you still let this guy take you for a cruise on his yacht, or whatever it is he has in mind? I mean, you *are* getting off on this, aren't you?"

Darien wanted to say no, that it was strictly business, but her innate desire to tell the truth made her hesitate. "I'm not sure," she said.

Virginia shook her head incredulously. "Phew. Maybe I'm a pervert, but I could see myself hopping in the sack with that guy pretty damned quick—assuming you're describing him like he is, of course."

"You're a prisoner of your fantasies the same as everybody else, Virginia."

"That's what it is, huh?" She popped her gum loudly.

"Look at it this way, I spent an evening with the guy and I don't feel I know him at all. Not really."

The receptionist grinned. "Maybe I'm easier to please."

Darien wanted to say, "Or maybe you haven't had the perfect life blow up in your face, like I did when the man I loved died." But she didn't. For all she knew, Virginia had had her own Todd and had experienced the pain of losing him just as she had.

Virginia gave Darien an uncertain look, then leaned into the cubicle, lowering her voice. "I wasn't going to tell you this until after I see how it works out, but thanks to you I might have started my own little fantasy adventure. A few weeks ago I met this guy at a party. Not Mr. Wonderful, but he might be a Mr. Tonight, if you get my drift. He's straight, divorced, of course, but no kids. No Adonis, either, but he's kind of cute and sexy in his own way."

"He asked you out?"

Virginia glanced around to make sure no one was within earshot. "I asked him. You gave me the courage to go after him, Darien. He's coming over for dinner this weekend. I'm buying a can of Hershey's syrup and keeping it on the nightstand, just in case."

With that bit of intelligence, Virginia headed toward her desk. Darien just sat there with a dazed expression on her face, her mind turning to Sam and apple brown Betty and whipped cream.

DARIEN POPPED the last french fry into her mouth and looked at Bob Smits. They had gone to lunch at the grill around the corner to talk about her next article.

"If you don't hear from him again, you can always write about your feelings about that. Or would that embarrass you?" he asked.

She shook her head. "Not really. I took to heart what you told me about putting more emotion into my writing. Now, if I don't let it all hang out, I almost feel dishonest."

"It shows, Darien, believe me!"

He was being complimentary, so she smiled. Then she finished the rest of her iced tea. Bob Smits looked at her as though he was trying to understand what or who he was really seeing. She noticed that lots of people had begun looking at her differently. At first she'd assumed it was the novelty of the situation, but as time went on she began to think there was more to it than that.

Bob had finished eating and he pushed his plate away, tucking his napkin under the edge of it. "You know something," he said, "I hadn't realized just how good these articles of yours were until Janet made a remark at breakfast the other day. She admitted she'd been thinking about Sam—how mysterious, sexy and romantic he is, how refreshing. And then, to top it off," he said, blushing, "that night for dinner she made this whipped cream and fruit and Grand Marnier thing. I, er, let's say she made me feed it to her."

He grinned self-consciously. "You know what went through my mind afterward, Darien? I wondered how many times that little scene has been played out around the Bay Area the past few days. I mean, if you had Janet making me whipped cream desserts, how many other women . . . well, you get the point."

"I know I'm supposed to be pleased about that," she said, "but for some reason I'm not—at least, not as much as I should be. Oh, I'm glad I've got an audience, of course. And I'm glad my writing is appreciated. But if you want to know the truth, Bob, sometimes I feel like I've been prostituting myself."

"Prostituting?"

"Well, maybe that's a bit too strong. I feel like an exhibitionist, like I'm Madonna baring her breasts in public, or something."

He chuckled. "You've touched a chord in people, all right, but there's no reason to assume the worst. Good journalism should be stimulating as well as informative."

"I bet Geraldo says the same thing every morning when he looks in the mirror."

"Look, Darien," Bob said, "have you been dishonest with your readers?"

"No."

"Case closed."

The waiter came with their bill. Bob picked up the check and they both walked over to the cashier. As he waited for his change, Darien looked around at her public, thinking about her boss's last remark. Honesty. Was honesty really the issue? she wondered.

They left the restaurant, strolling along the crowded sidewalk in silence. San Francisco was a wonderfully diverse city. It was sophisticated and cosmopolitan. People from all over the world appreciated the variety it had to offer culturally. Yet there was another dimension to San Francisco she hadn't thought about—or even recognized—when she'd decided to move here. It was the dark side of the city, the side that championed sexual freedom, danger, living on the edge. New York had had a dark side, too, but it hadn't lured her the same way, challenged her to take risks.

She shook her head. Maybe she was letting her fantasies get to her. Or maybe it was because she was thirty now. Perhaps the city wasn't truly different. Perhaps *she* was different. All she knew for certain was that something about that dark side called to her, made her want to challenge and explore, dare to take her dreams to the limit. She'd been honest about that. Maybe Bob was right. Maybe that was the extent of her obligation.

She glanced at the sky. It was still overcast but a bit warmer than it had been that morning. She was glad she'd left her sweater in the office.

"What can I expect in the next installment?" Bob asked. "Have you finished your piece for tomorrow?"

They'd gotten through the entire lunch without tomorrow having come up. Since she was up in the air about it, she hadn't wanted to discuss it. But it was natural that Bob would want to know.

"No," she replied, "I'm still struggling with it. This morning I wrote about a thousand words on what it was like to wait around, hoping my next fantasy would come true." Darien chuckled. "Then I wrote another thousand on what it was like to hope it didn't come true."

Bob laughed. "That sounds good to me. There's not a person in San Francisco who couldn't identify with one or both of those themes. One of the biggest fears most folks have is what they'd do if all their wishes suddenly came true. The way Janet puts it is, always be careful what you wish for, in case you get it."

They turned the corner. The office was on Battery Street, about half a block away. Darien was rolling Bob's last words through her mind. He was right. Dead right. What a fabulous idea! "That's it! Bob, you're a genius. Or maybe Janet is!"

He blinked. "How so?"

"What you just said. Everybody has something they dream about, and you're right, a lot of people would rather have their dream stay a fantasy, where it's nice and safe, because reality never quite lives up to the dream— it can't. To tell you the truth, that's one of the reasons I hesitated about going to Perry's to meet Sam. I was afraid I'd be disillusioned."

"But you weren't."

"True. But it's still early. The point is, I know what I want to say in my next article. The beauty of it is it doesn't matter whether Sam contacts me or not. And *that's* a hundred percent honest!"

They came to the *Bulletin* building. Bob, who was ruminating on what she'd said, silently opened the door and they headed for the elevator. After Darien pushed the up button they both stood there, waiting. When the car arrived and the door opened, Darien recalled how surprised she'd been when Sam had been in the elevator the day he'd come to the paper. But this time it was empty—no Sam. Nobody at all. The twinge of disappointment she felt made her wonder if her expressed indifference was as honest as she'd thought.

They got in the elevator for the ride to the third floor. When the door opened they were surprised to see that most of the people were away from their desks. Instead of the usual hubbub there was a strange quiet in the vast room. Everyone had crowded over in the far corner where Darien's cubicle was located.

She turned to Bob, but he shrugged his shoulders. "Come on," he said, "let's see what's going on."

They made their way across the room, weaving in and out of the aisles between partitions. The closer they got to Darien's cubicle, the more sure she was that whatever had grabbed people's attention had to do with her.

They saw Virginia standing next to Carolyn Buchanan. The receptionist giggled as they approached. "My God, Darien. You won't believe it. I mean, you *really* won't believe it!"

Darien turned to Carolyn, but she was trying to keep from giggling herself. "Just go to your desk," was all she said.

Everyone started parting to let her and Bob through. Then suddenly the last two people moved from in front of her cubicle and Darien saw him—a huge muscular black man dressed like some sort of ancient Egyptian standing directly in front her desk. He wore leather sandals and had on one of those little pleated short skirts with the big scarf headgear like King Tut wore in the movies. He was holding a golden box in his hand. On closer inspection, she saw that it was a miniature replica of King Tut's sarcophagus.

He looked at her, his face an implacable mask. "Darien Hughes?"

She nodded.

"My master asked that you accept this." He handed over the golden box and then bowed. "What you seek is inside."

Darien swallowed hard. The box wasn't heavy. She shook it, but she felt too embarrassed to open it then, with half the news staff looking on. She looked at Bob beseechingly and he seemed to understand. "All right, everybody," he said, "time to get back to work. Show's over."

There was a collective sigh, then everyone began to drift back to their desks. Rob Barker was one of the last to go. "Not bad, if you like theater," he said. "I wonder what Prince Charming has in mind. A little cruise down the Nile, maybe?"

Darien gave him a dirty look. "I don't know that this is from Sam. It could be from somebody else."

"Yeah, sure. Like maybe Osgood over in the travel section has the hots for you and this is his way of letting you know." Rod chuckled, but Darien didn't think it was funny. Everyone knew that Osgood Kingsbury was gay.

Finally Rob left and she was alone with Bob Smits and the messenger. "Would you like to open that in my office?" Bob asked. "At least that way you'd have a little privacy."

"I'll take you up on that," Darien said. She turned to the man in the Egyptian costume. "Thank you for bringing this."

He nodded. "I am to wait here for your response."

Darien told him she'd return in a few minutes, then she followed Bob to his office. When they got there he closed the door and she set the box on the corner of his desk. Darien looked at him tentatively before she opened it. Inside was a scroll. The writing was done in calligraphy and the edge of the scroll was decorated in hieroglyphics. Sam had gone to a lot of trouble.

Darien, the pleasure of your company is requested this weekend at the Luxor Hotel in Las Vegas. There will be a first-class plane ticket in your name waiting at the airport. A suite has been reserved for you, and all your expenses will be taken care of. As for the rest, well, let's just say you'll have to trust me.

                                                    Sam

Darien handed the scroll to Bob without saying a word. When he had finished reading it, he smiled. "I don't know whether you want to go or not, but this would make one hell of a story. I'll say one thing for this guy...he has imagination."

But Darien scarcely heard him. Her mind was on the comment Janet Smits had made about being careful what you wish for because it might come true. Sam's invitation had brought all her doubts and fears to the surface again. It was the moment of truth.

"You don't look very happy," Bob said.

"I know you like this from a journalistic perspective," she said, "but if I was your daughter or your sister, how would you feel about it?"

"You're putting me on the spot," he said.

"I put myself on the spot by getting involved. Now I'm having doubts."

He studied her, folding his arms over his chest as he sat on the edge of his desk. "I can't advise you on this, Darien. Only you can decide what you're going to do."

She nodded. Had Sam taken to heart what she'd written in her second article about putting her interests first? He knew that winning her trust was key. But would he be so cynical as to try to take advantage of misplaced trust? Or was this guy, whoever he really was, Sam at heart—her fantasy man who understood her needs and knew exactly what to do?

Bob continued to watch her. "Maybe I *do* have some responsibility for this," he said. "I'm not going to have one of my best reporters ruined by a story. If this thing is getting to you, maybe it's better if you quit. God knows there's plenty out there to write about besides this."

His reaction surprised her. And it also pleased her that he should care. "You want me to drop it?"

"I want you to do what's best for you."

She went over to the window, still badly in need of washing, and watched as a couple of pigeons fluttered past, eventually landing on a sill on the building across the street. "If I quit, the whole Bay area will consider it a cop-out."

"They have no way of knowing what Sam proposed."

"But *I* do, Bob, and I'm honest—too damned honest for my own good, probably."

He said nothing for a minute, then spoke. "So what are you going to tell King Tut out there?"

Darien turned from the window. "That I'm going, of course." She gave him an ironic smile. "I have but one body to give for my paper. And I might as well do it at somebody else's expense."

6

"YOU KNOW what scares me most?" Darien said at dinner that night. "I'm not sure why I'm doing this."

She was in Maryanne's kitchen, sitting at the tiny oak drop-leaf table and waiting for her friend to sit down. They tried to get together about once a week for dinner, usually trading off who cooked, though occasionally they'd go out. Darien liked it best when they did that because neither of them was very talented in the kitchen.

"Why do you think you're doing it?" Maryanne asked, pulling her chair up to the table.

Darien considered the question as she poked her fork at her friend's latest creation, a vegetarian casserole made with tofu, crushed potato chips, mushroom soup, carrots, celery and leftover peas. It tasted as bland as it looked. "Partly for the sake of my job, though that's not the main reason. Something's driving me. It's not curiosity, it's not even lust. It's a... I don't know, a compulsion, I suppose."

"What sort of compulsion?"

"I don't want to say a sort of death wish, because I have no desire to get hurt, but the pull seems sinister, somehow. It's like I crave the danger Sam represents. Does that make sense?"

"Yes, actually." Maryanne took a sip of tea. "Jung talked about the shadow side of things. There are degrees of danger in nearly everything, Darien. Adventure, sex, you name it. Even creativity involves risk. It's inner tension that motivates people to do things."

"You're trying to say Sam is good for me."

"He could be," Maryanne said. "At least what he represents."

"And just what do you think he represents?"

"Feelings. Desires you've been denying, maybe. The mind will seize upon things and then turn them to its purpose. Our subconscious can be amazingly wise."

"How about foolish?" Darien asked.

"Our creative impulses have to be tempered with judgment, it's true. That's the key to successful living— knowing how and where to strike the balance."

"That sounds kind of clinical, if you don't mind me saying so."

Maryanne grinned broadly. She had on the linen dress she'd worn to work. Her strawberry curls were windblown and she hadn't bothered to brush her hair since getting to her apartment, though she had removed her jacket and beret before starting dinner. Darien's contribution had been to drink a glass of wine while she watched Maryanne cook.

"The point I'm trying to make is that there can be good reasons for your compulsions," Maryanne said.

"Maybe," Darien said, "but there are good reasons I shouldn't be playing this game, too."

"Such as?"

"I know damned well Sam is going to try to seduce me—I'd bet my life on it. I can't say he's completely cynical, he may even have genuine concern for my happiness and well-being, but..."

"But what?"

"I'm afraid that being seduced is exactly what I want. Let's face it, this thing with Sam is a sexual fantasy, and that's just fine with me."

"Is it really?"

"Yes. And no. How I feel depends on whether I'm in my fantasy mode or my common sense mode."

"I can understand that. But so far your fantasies haven't been self-destructive," Maryanne said. "If they had been, I'd be worried. But as long as you stay in control, everything should be all right."

"Maybe that's what I'm really afraid of," Darien said. "Losing control. Maybe *wanting* to lose control!" She took another bite of casserole.

Maryanne added some more hot tea to her cup and took a sip. As she put down her cup, she reached over and touched Darien's arm. "Even though that may be a part of the fantasy, it doesn't necessarily mean you'll do it when push comes to shove. You're not weak, Darien. If you were the type of woman who was easily manipulated, incapable of asserting herself, I'd counsel against this trip. But you aren't like that. I'd trust your willpower over my own."

Darien squeezed Maryanne's hand. "Thanks for saying that."

"It's true."

"Maybe. But you know the real irony? I feel just a little bit decadent. That's a side of me I didn't even know existed, and now it's pulling me toward this fantasy."

Maryanne gazed at her, her expression turning serious. "I kind of wish you hadn't said that."

Darien laughed. "Well, it's too late now. I'm going off to the Luxor in Vegas to meet my destiny!"

AT NINE O'CLOCK Saturday morning Darien locked the front door of her cottage and started down the pathway carrying her suitcase. As she walked past the blooming rosebushes she inhaled deeply, savoring the heady fragrance. The garden seemed safe and secure, especially in contrast to the adventure she was about to embark on. For three long days she'd agonized. Of course, the good news was that she'd used her turmoil as grist for her journalistic mill.

She had written about her struggle to find the fine line between impulse and reason. Every woman alive understood that one. How much danger did one risk in pursuit of pleasure? Only the most foolhardy leaped forward blindly. Sam, it seemed, had understood that, too. He'd made it easy for her to say yes. But that also was a good reason for concern. She had ended her piece with a cliffhanger—poised at the point of going off to Vegas to meet a mysterious stranger she knew only as Sam.

Darien set down her bag to close the gate. The taxi hadn't arrived, but that was okay. Knowing she'd have to pick up her plane ticket, she had allowed plenty of time to get to the airport.

She'd never been to Las Vegas, but she'd been imprinted with the images she'd seen in films and magazines over the years. She was also aware that it had recently become a lot more than a gambling town whose signature was a long-legged show girl with bare breasts. Still, its image was of a place where desires, especially darker desires, were the order of the day—and the night.

Darien couldn't help wondering if by choosing Las Vegas Sam wasn't sending the message that it was his kind of town. For all she knew he was a regular, a high roller who went there often to party, perhaps with a different companion each time. If so, she hoped it would become apparent sooner rather than later.

Darien checked her watch, then glanced at the house. There was no sign of Marc or Dean, though she half expected them to be at the window, as if secretly watching their child going off for her first day of school. They'd had her over for dinner the night before. Marc had made a fabulous seven-layer spinach lasagna with four different cheeses. They'd had a mixed green salad and sourdough bread and a lovely lemon soufflé for dessert.

They hadn't talked about her trip as they ate, but as soon as they were finished Marc served after-dinner drinks in the living room as a sort of prelude to getting down to business.

While Dean sat silently, obviously determined to hold his tongue at all costs, she and Marc had discussed clothes. Marc insisted that Vegas was the sort of place where the more outrageous you were, the better.

"But Marc," she'd insisted, "I don't have clothes that are beaded or bangled or spangled."

"Well, sweetie, there must be something you could wear. I mean, forgive me, but a decent pair of slacks and a silk blouse won't cut it in a casino, especially if you're pretending to be a party girl."

"*Party* girl?"

"Well, that's the fantasy, isn't it? I mean, why are you going to Las Vegas, if it isn't to kick up your heels and have a good time?"

"Honestly, Marc," Dean said, with thinly disguised disgust, "to listen to you, one would think you're part of the grand conspiracy."

"What grand conspiracy?"

"The one this Sam concocted to lure Darien to Las Vegas to do . . . to do—"

"To do what?" Marc said, putting his hands on his hips.

"Whatever it is he has in mind!" Dean shot back.

"Like have a good time, maybe? *Fun?* Since when did partying a little become a sin?"

Dean rolled his eyes. "It's a wonder you survived to adulthood, Marc."

Marc touched Darien on the arm. "Don't listen to that man, sweetie. You're a big girl. You know what you're doing. You've got judgment and sense."

"I wish I could say the same about you," Dean groused.

"Well," Darien said, interrupting before the argument got in full swing, "you'll both be happy to know I intend to go to Vegas to have a good time, *and* so I can share it with my readers. And I'll exert both caution and good sense."

"See how easy it is to be reasonable?" Marc said to Dean, elevating his nose. "I told you Darien had a good head on her shoulders." He turned to her. "So, tell me, what *are* you taking to wear?"

She took a sip of her Amaretto. "I do have a sort of basic black dress. It's raw silk, has little cap sleeves."

Marc's expression was dubious.

"It has a scoop neck," she said hopefully.

"How scooped?"

"Not very."

He sighed. "Even with pearls and dark hose it sounds sort of . . . funeralesque."

Darien laughed. "I did wear it to a funeral once, as a matter of fact. With a little Chanel jacket I borrowed from a friend."

Marc snapped his fingers as if he'd just come up with a terrific idea. "Say, is there any chance you can get the paper to cough up the bread for a suitable dress? Some of the hotel shops are fabulous, and after all, the trip isn't costing the *Bulletin* a sou."

She nodded. "That's not a half-bad idea. The only problem is, I leave in the morning and there's no time to hit Bob for the extra money. Nice as it would be to dress up a little, I'm afraid I'm going to have to settle for looking like the humble reporter that I am."

"Well, that's hardly a disaster," Marc said charitably. "After all, it was the person you are that attracted Sam in the first place. Just be the sweet girl you are."

Darien smiled at the recollection. In different ways, they were both protective of her. That made her feel good, knowing they cared. Again she looked at the house, hoping for a good-luck wave, but there was still no sign of either them. Darien sighed, wishing she felt as confident as Marc about what she was about to do. At the same time, she figured it was probably good that she shared some of Dean's skepticism.

The taxi came around the corner and Darien felt a surge of adrenaline. Well, this was it! Thinking about it, she *did* feel like Alice about to visit Wonderland.

DARIEN looked out the window of the plane at the scorched brown earth of the Mojave Desert. In July it would be hot as blazes.

"Don't give it a thought," Marc had said at dinner the night before, "nobody ever goes outside in Las Vegas unless it's to get in a taxi to go to a show at a different hotel. And even at that it'll be night."

Darien had assumed as much. She knew that Las Vegas was awake twenty-four hours a day and that most people could scarcely tell the difference between two in the afternoon and two in the morning. Never having gambled, she wasn't sure if she'd get lost in time the way some people reportedly did, but she was prepared for a strange mixture of "Times Square and Disneyland rolled into one and put on the moon." That's the way Rod Barker described it the last time he'd dropped by her cubicle to leer and take a stab at being witty.

The plane was in its descent and Darien gazed wistfully at a highway far below. The narrow ribbon of blacktop stretched in a perfectly straight line from one end of the desert valley to the other. The only break in the landscape, apart from the parched mountains on the horizon, was an occasional building, a metal roof gleaming in the sun, or a stand of trees along the roadside.

As they continued their descent, signs of civilization began to multiply. Clusters of buildings got larger, becoming hamlets and towns. Soon they were over the outskirts of Las Vegas. After making a sweeping circle of McCarran International, the jet glided down, touching the ground with a gentle bump.

As she came out of the jetway and into the terminal, the first thing Darien saw was a bank of slot machines. It brought home the fact that she was in a different world, one where the normal rules of everyday life no longer applied.

She spotted an attractive dark-haired young woman who was holding a sign that said, "Ms. Hughes."

"Welcome to Las Vegas," the woman said when Darien introduced herself. "I'm Adrianne DiMarco, with the Luxor. I'll be escorting you to the hotel."

"How nice."

"It's not the usual procedure," she said with a smile, "but you're a special guest. Did you have a good flight?"

"Yes, thank you. Very nice."

Adrianne led the way to the tram, which they rode to the main terminal building. They were met in the baggage claim area by a chauffeur who carried Darien's luggage to a white limousine waiting just outside the door. The air outdoors was hot and dry, but the interior of the limo was cool. The leather of the seat felt almost cold to the touch.

"Have you been to the Luxor before?" Adrianne asked.

"No, this is my first trip to Las Vegas, as a matter of fact."

"Oh, then you're in for a treat. We at the Luxor like to think we have one of the most exotic tourist destinations in the country. Did you see the pyramid from the air, by any chance?"

"No, mostly I saw mountains."

"You were on the wrong side of the plane, apparently. The hotel is a thirty-story pyramid. I don't know if you were aware of that."

"I was aware of the Egyptian theme, of course."

"It's quite a spectacular property," she said. "There's a ten-story replica of the great sphinx, and a one-hundred-and-ninety-foot Egyptian obelisk out front. The pyramid is easily seen from the air. In fact, the beam of light shining from the top at night is the most powerful in the world. Pilots say it can be seen all the way from Los Angeles at cruising altitude."

"I had no idea there was anything like this out here."

"Your host was most insistent that this be a very special experience for you, Ms. Hughes."

"Do you know Sam?"

The woman betrayed a slight smile. "Not personally, no."

Darien wondered if there was something being left unsaid. She had no reason to feel leery on the basis of her reaction, but she couldn't help being a little uncomfortable not knowing for sure what she was getting into.

"Do you know Sam by reputation, then?" Darien asked.

"I don't mean to be evasive," Adrianne replied, "but my instructions were not to discuss him."

"I see." Darien remained silent as the limo whisked along the main boulevard. She glanced out the window, seeing new buildings on the fringe of the city rising from the expanse of sagebrush. "I didn't expect this at all," Darien said.

"It's quite something, isn't it," Adrianne DiMarco said. "Now, if you need anything, please don't hesitate to ask. The first priority is to pamper you, provide anything and everything you wish."

"Anything?"

She nodded.

"Do you provide the gambling money, too?" Darien asked with a laugh.

"Actually, a three-thousand dollar credit line has been established in your name, Ms. Hughes. If you require more, let me know."

Darien blinked. "You're kidding."

"No. Everything at the Luxor is free to you. Well, there is undoubtedly a limit on the credit line, but I'm certain it's substantial. Once you're registered, I'll see to it you have a special card that will make anything and everything you want available to you."

Darien was beginning to see just how fantastic this fantasy was proving to be. Sam had outdone himself. He'd even made the hotel staff his coconspirators. "Is this red carpet treatment something you're called on to do often?" she asked.

"We do have special guests with special needs from time to time, but it's certainly not routine."

"I see."

"Is there a problem?" Adrianne asked with concern.

"No, it all seems a bit too good to be true."

"I think you'll find the Luxor very real and very exciting."

"I already do, and we aren't even there yet." Darien glanced out the window as they drove past the MGM Grand. She'd read in the flight magazine that it was the largest hotel in the world. Directly across the street was the Tropicana, and catercorner from the MGM was the Excalibur with its fairy-castle spires.

The limo turned onto Las Vegas Boulevard. The obelisk and the sphinx, surrounded by green tufted palms brushing the sky, came into view, and then the black pyramid itself. As they drew closer, Darien was taken aback by its size. The sphinx appeared as it must have looked three thousand years earlier, when it was new and freshly painted.

The limousine went up the sweeping drive, past cascading fountains to the covered entry at the base of the pyramid. They disembarked and entered the soaring atrium of the pyramid.

Indoors it was cool and lush with palms. The stark white walls, honeycombed with guest rooms, sloped inward and upward on all four sides to the misty heights of the apex.

After she'd registered, Adrianne asked if she wanted to go directly to her suite or if she preferred to take a tour of the facility.

"I think I'd like to freshen up," Darien told her, "and then wander around on my own later."

Together they went to the bank of inclinators. Since the walls sloped inward as well as upward, a traditional elevator wouldn't have worked. The inclinator went sideways and up at the same time. Darien found the sensation odd, but not unpleasant.

They stopped on the twenty-eighth floor. Adrianne led the way along the maroon, turquoise and white-carpeted hallway. The plaster walls bore life-size, traditional-style paintings of Egyptian kings and queens. Coming to Darien's suite, Adrianne opened the door.

There was a short hallway with a stone floor. A half bath was to her right, and just ahead, on the left, was a wet bar, a big one with a small kitchen area. Straight ahead was a sitting room with a dining table and chairs. The bedroom and bath were past the sitting room on the right. Everything faced the slanting windows that overlooked much of Las Vegas.

Darien couldn't believe it. There were fragments of wall paintings over the red and gold sofa, and the tall columns that separated the bar from the dining area were covered in black and white hieroglyphics.

"There's an envelope for you on the coffee table," Adrianne said, gesturing toward it. "I'll leave you now, but if I can be of help in any way, please give me a call." Smiling, she handed Darien her card. "I hope you enjoy your stay."

Once the woman had gone, Darien went over to the table and snatched up the envelope, opening it nervously. Inside was a neatly typed note.

Darien,
I hope the accommodations meet with your approval. As a lover of cultural anthropology and history, I find the Luxor especially delightful. Per-

haps you will, as well.

If I may, I'll come by your suite this evening at 7:30. Perhaps we can have a drink before dining at the Ibis. I don't know about you, but I've always had a passion for evening clothes. In case you didn't bring formal wear, I arranged to have Chantal's, one of the nicer boutiques in town, leave a few dresses for you to have a look at. They are in the wardrobe in the bedroom. If none of their selections meet with your approval, or if you need accessories, give them a call. Their card is enclosed.

Meanwhile, the afternoon is yours. Whatever you do, indulge yourself. I shall do my best to make your fantasy weekend as pleasurable as possible. See you this evening. Enjoy.

Sam

Darien glanced over the note again, then put it down. This was proving to be Christmas, Valentine's Day and graduation all wrapped into one. Sam was trying hard to be unthreatening, to make her feel at ease. That was evident. Ironically, it was having the opposite effect. She felt a little like she was being led down the primrose path. Thirty years had tempered the child in her. This *was* too good to be true. There was a catch, and it would become evident before the night was over.

Darien knew when she accepted the invitation to Las Vegas that the time would come when she'd have to deal with Sam. It didn't have to be unpleasant. It might even be enjoyable, just as their dinner at Perry's had been. It all depended on Sam.

Meanwhile, though, she'd make the most of the opportunity he'd given her. Her readers were counting on her. Though she had misgivings, it was hard not to fall into the spirit of the adventure. Feeling cautiously optimistic, she went off to the bedroom to see what sort of dresses she had to choose from.

There were four in the armoire, and all of them were her size. That made her wonder all the more about Sam. How many men, even a married man, knew anything about women's dress sizes? Not many, that was certain. Which meant that Sam either had an incredibly good eye and had had a hell of a lot of practice doing this sort of thing, or he was lucky. She wouldn't have bet on the latter.

The first dress was an electric blue, low-cut and completely beaded. It wasn't her kind of thing so she didn't even bother to try it on. The next two were black. One was cut low in the back, the other in the front. But the fourth dress really caught her eye. It was red silk, strapless and very plain—no beads or bows or pleats, just gorgeous fabric and clean lines.

Darien quickly took off the tan cotton safari dress she'd worn on the plane. She hadn't brought a strapless bra along, so she tried the dress on without one. As soon as she zipped the dress up the back, she knew it was the one she wanted. It fit beautifully. The waist was defined and the skirt was slim and straight with a slit up the back, though not too far. She'd brought along black heels and hose, and they'd be great with it.

Darien went to the bathroom to look at herself in the mirror. She stood on her toes to get the effect of heels. The dress was a bit too long, but with high heels she ought to be all right. She turned sideways, then looked at herself straight on.

She looked okay. In fact, she looked terrific. All her life she'd wondered what she'd look like in a dress this sophisticated. Not that it was daring, because it wasn't.

The gown didn't even show a hint of cleavage. But the color and cut made her feel like a woman of the world, a woman who had been on a lot of adventures and was about to embark on another one.

Darien carefully slipped the dress off and hung it in the armoire. Then she started to unpack. By the time she finished she was starting to droop. She hadn't slept much the past few nights—she'd been too excited thinking about what might happen this weekend.

She plopped down on the bed to plan the afternoon. A facial, some time in the sauna and a massage would probably be a good way to start. She'd have to call the beauty salon to get an appointment for her hair and nails. After all that, if there was enough time, a nap would be welcome.

Then, that evening, she'd put on the red dress and her high heels and maybe some glitzy earrings, if she could find some in one of the hotel shops. And when Sam showed up, she'd let him show her around. It would be as good a way as any to begin their fantasy.

7

FOR THE PAST five minutes Darien had been pacing, going from the mirror in the bath to the one behind the bar, evaluating her image. Even to her critical eye, she knew she looked good—chic and sexy. Almost as if she'd been transformed into a woman from another time. Suddenly it hit her. It had been eight years since she'd had on a floor-length gown. That occasion couldn't have been more different.

A year after Todd died, she'd gone down to Newport to be a bridesmaid at the wedding of Julie Bellingham, her roommate in college. Despite the gaiety, Darien just couldn't forget that Julie had expected her to be *matron* of honor when the date was originally set. Todd's accident had changed that.

The best man, a nice-looking law student with horn-rimmed glasses who was named Ryan something or other, had been the best friend of the groom, Carter Pearson, all through prep school and college. Julie had hoped Ryan might draw Darien out of her shell, but it was not to be. A relationship was the last thing Darien had wanted.

For a few years after that she'd occasionally hear something about Ryan from Julie. Both he and Carter were working their way up the partnership ladder in prestigious Manhattan firms. Julie continued to hope until Ryan finally married and the issue became moot. By the time Darien had left New York, Julie had become a suburban Connecticut housewife and mother of two little boys.

In the past year she'd only seen Julie once—when they'd met for lunch in Manhattan to say goodbye before Darien moved to San Francisco. Since then they'd exchanged Christmas cards, but that was it.

Darien thought about how far she'd come from the days when she'd been on the verge of getting married herself. If Todd hadn't been killed, the two of them might be spending this weekend in New York—meeting Julie and Carter for dinner at Tavern on the Green—or going to their place in Connecticut. Instead Darien found herself in a sumptuous suite atop a magical pyramid in the Mojave Desert, waiting for a mysterious man to take her off for a fantasy evening.

Darien heard a knock and quickly made her way through the suite to open the door. Sam was standing there in a tuxedo and black tie. He looked devastatingly handsome, his expression bemused. He proceeded to look her over, taking his time.

"You look absolutely stunning," he said.

"Thanks, Professor Higgins." She gestured for him to come in.

As he entered, he paused to brush his cheek against hers and inhale her scent. "Hmm, you smell good, too."

The gesture was unexpected. She repressed a shiver as she closed the door and followed him to the sitting room. He was glancing around.

"How are the digs? Are you comfortable?"

"Very. But isn't it a bit ostentatious? An ordinary room would have been fine."

"Somehow ordinary doesn't go with my conception of you," he said easily. "Nor do I want it to go with your conception of me."

"Oh? And why is that?"

"Fantasies should be special and I intend for this weekend to be very special."

Darien wasn't sure if she heard something vaguely ominous in his tone, or if it was all in her head. "Perhaps I'm more easily impressed than you think."

He shook his head. "I don't think so. You're a woman of taste, class, sophistication, savoir faire . . ."

She held up her hand to stop him. "You know how to flatter, too. Is it part of the act, or is it you?"

He gave her an enigmatic smile. "What do you want it to be?"

Darien could see he was taking the game seriously, pulling out all the stops. She wasn't sure what the implications of that were, but one thing was certain. Sam had her where he wanted her—in a hotel suite five hundred miles from home.

"Do you want a drink?" she asked, determined not to panic.

"If you do."

"I haven't even looked to see what's in the bar," she said, moving toward it.

"I'll get the drinks," he said, stopping her. "You relax."

Darien sat on the red and black and white striped couch. She crossed her legs.

"Scotch, vodka, gin, rum, bourbon, Canadian, dry sherry and a variety of mixes," Sam reported. "What's your pleasure?"

"A little sherry would be nice. Please."

Sam moved behind the bar as though he knew what he was doing. She heard the tinkle of ice cubes.

"Do you come to Vegas often?" she asked.

"Do you really want me to answer that?"

"Are you suggesting the rules of the game prohibit any questions at all?"

"I could answer you easily, but do you really want to know all about me? I would think the more mysterious I am, the more powerful the effect. And the better your next article. That is what this is all about, isn't it?"

He moved behind the large pictograph-covered pillar at the corner of the bar.

"Forgive the skepticism, Sam, but your dedication to journalism is somehow . . ."

"Somehow what?"

"Suspect."

"The result should be all that matters," he said as he peered around the pillar at her. "Or have you gotten cold feet?" He came out of the bar carrying two glasses—a sherry for her and a whiskey over ice for him. He handed hers over and dropped smoothly onto the sofa next to her. "Is that it?"

"I guess I'm having problems with the fact that we have such an unequal relationship," she said, looking him dead in the eye. "You know all about me, yet I know nothing about you."

"Mystique," he said. "Elixir for the romantic soul."

"My, but aren't we waxing poetic?"

"I've been practicing," he said with a sly wink.

"You know, I bet you have."

"I'm determined that you get your money's worth."

"Glad you didn't say *your* money's worth."

He gave her a sardonic look. "That might happen, too. Who knows?" He extended his glass toward hers. "To the loveliest creature this side of the Nile, bar none."

She sipped a little sherry. "Tell me, do you take women to exotic places to play games frequently, or is this new for you?"

He stroked his chin. "Darien, you seem intent on unmasking me. Tell you what. You can ask me three questions about myself each day we're together—any three questions you want, so long as they can be answered yes or no."

"My, how generous of you." She had more sherry.

"Do you want this to be your first?" he asked.

Darien shook her head. "No, if you're going to be stingy, I'm going to have to make my questions count."

"You're wise. Pick your shots carefully." He leaned back, sighing contentedly. His gaze settled on her legs. "So, you found a dress that pleases you?"

"Yes. It was very generous of you," she replied. "Thank you very much."

"I didn't tell you we'd be dressing before you left because I didn't want you to feel you had to run out and buy something. Making it my treat seemed more considerate. Besides, I think it pleases me even more than it pleases you, if you want to know the truth."

She studied him. "You're enjoying this power you have, aren't you, Sam?"

He sloshed his drink around in his glass, giving her a mischievous grin. "I enjoy the company, Darien. I enjoy you."

"And do you enjoy buying clothes for women, making them feel . . . kept?"

"Is that intended to be your first question?"

"Grump," she said, giving him a look.

"I'll give you a freebie," he said. "The answer is yes, I like buying things for women."

"Then you must do it often."

"Statements that are really questions ought to be counted," he said.

"You're a hard man." She took a sip of sherry.

"Just to show what a sport I am, I'll give you another free one. The answer is no, not often."

"Rags like this will put a dent in the old budget," she said, "so I hope for your sake it's not too often."

"I won't be skipping any meals."

He put his hand on her knee. Darien looked down at it, feeling the heat of his palm right through the silk. She didn't say anything, but she continued to stare at his hand, hoping he'd get the message. After a moment or two, he squeezed her knee and then removed his hand.

"Would you care to hear about the evening I've planned?" he said smoothly, as if he hadn't noticed her rather pointed hint.

"Certainly."

"I thought we could have a leisurely dinner and then take in the late show. It's colorful, entertaining."

"I'd like that."

"And later, there's the casino, if that sort of thing appeals to you."

"I've never gambled before," she told him. "Not seriously. When I was in college some friends and I went to Atlantic City. We played nickel slot machines."

He chuckled. "You can move up to quarters, if you think you could handle the pressure."

"Don't be snide. And by the way, what's this credit line they told me about? You weren't serious about that, were you?"

"Sure," he said, drawing on his drink, "why not?"

"Because it's excessive, that's why."

"Excessive by what standard?"

"Evidently not by yours," she said dryly. Then she gave him a penetrating look. "Do you think you're going to buy me?"

He gave her a sideward glance. "Do you want to be bought?"

"Of course not!"

"Then there's your answer. Making like a high-priced call girl is not in your repertoire of fantasies. And the only things that will work in this fantasy, Darien, are the ones that please you. My job is to find them."

She gave him a wary look. "I think you're having too much fun with this," she said.

"To the contrary, discovering your secret fantasies is not an easy task. But I'll do my best...whatever it takes."

"If that's an oblique reference to anything kinky, you can forget it. That's not my style. I'm not here for sex," she said defensively. "Though I'm starting to think you are. Come clean, Sam. What are you up to? What do you want? Really."

"That's not a question that can be answered yes or no."

She grimaced and looked at her sherry glass and thought for a moment. "All right, here's my first question. Did you bring me here with the intention of seducing me?"

"No."

She gave him a skeptical look. "Why don't I believe you?"

"You probably feel safer thinking the worst." He paused. "I'll confess to this much—I wouldn't be a normal red-blooded male if romance didn't cross my mind when I'm around you. But I didn't bring you here with any specific intent."

"You're too damned smooth for your own good. Or mine!"

He seemed genuinely amused.

"Well, are you?" she asked.

"Is that your second question?"

"No!"

He took her hand, pulled her fingers to his lips and kissed them. "You're a delight."

"And *you're* infuriating!"

He chuckled. "Why? Because I'm enjoying myself? Anyway, I'm only doing what I promised. I hope you're taking notes, by the way. Thousands of readers back home are waiting expectantly to hear all about this."

"They won't be hearing about your conquest, I assure you!"

He opened his mouth to respond, but thought better of it and held his tongue.

"What were you going to say?" she said. "You censored it."

"Never mind."

"No, I want to hear. The spontaneous response is usually the honest one."

"All right. I was about to say, the lady doth protest too much. There, are you happy?"

Darien turned bright red, probably as red as the dress. She gulped some sherry. "Sam. If you truly understood women, you'd realize that by coming here I've put myself in a precarious position. It's only natural that I'd feel defensive."

"I was making an observation, not a criticism. The truth is, I admire your adventurous spirit."

He looked her over, just as he had before. Darien wasn't absolutely sure if Sam her fantasy man was talking, or if it was the flesh and blood man who'd suggested they extend the game. In a way she supposed it didn't matter, because right now, for this weekend at least, they were one and the same.

When she didn't say anything, Sam finally said, "If you're still concerned about my motives, look at it this way. I get to be an eyewitness to what everybody in the Bay Area is waiting to experience vicariously. Additionally, I get to . . . well, let's say participate."

"That's it? You're saying all this money you've spent is just to be an eyewitness?"

"Is that your second question?" he asked.

"No! I'm saving my last two."

Sam grinned. Darien took another drink of her sherry, then looked at his watch.

"When's dinner?"

"We have a while. Is there something you'd like to do first, anything in the hotel you haven't seen?"

"Actually, about all I've seen is the spa. I thought I'd let you give me a tour, since this seems to be your turf."

The corners of his mouth curled. "I'd be honored."

Sam got up, offering her his hand. Darien took it, and as he helped her to her feet, she noticed that he inhaled her scent again. It wasn't subtle, nor did she think it was intended to be. He even gave a little smile of pleasure as if to signal his approval.

Sam didn't let go of her immediately. She became aware of the warmth of his skin and the possessive way he kept hold of her hand. She hated to admit it, but despite her defensiveness, she was beginning to enjoy the game.

THEY EXITED the inclinator and Sam offered Darien his arm. They were a good deal more dressed up than most of the people they saw, but she didn't care. She was in a beautiful gown on the arm of a devastatingly handsome man, and in the process of building a fantasy. She decided to throw herself into the game.

They went to the attraction level at the base of the atrium first. The theme was high-tech futuristic, a paradox considering the Luxor was inspired by ancient Egypt. Yet it worked. Rising from the floor of the atrium was a stylized city of terra-cotta and slate-colored skyscrapers housing cafés, bars and shops.

Darien and Sam had more than a few admiring glances. One little girl, probably thinking they were part of the attraction, asked Darien if she could have her autograph to show her friends at home.

Sam grinned as Darien accommodated her, signing a postcard of the Luxor pyramid. When the child scampered off, he chuckled.

"At the rate you're going, you may be discovered by a talent agent before the night is over."

"I'm afraid I have absolutely no talent for acting, so there's not much chance of that," she said. "Besides, even if Hollywood beckoned, I'm hardly in your league."

"A compliment?" he said, squeezing her hand.

"You'll have to decide for yourself."

They went to the casino. Sam said they had a few minutes before their reservation at the Isis, so they paused to watch the table games. The excitement centered around the crap tables, but the crowd was such they couldn't get close enough to see much. After a while they came to a table where only a few men and one woman were playing.

They watched an attractive woman in her late thirties blow on the dice and toss them the length of the table.

"Seven, winner seven," the stick man intoned.

Darien watched stacks of chips move across the table as the dealers paid off bets. The dice were returned to the shooter and the woman threw craps three, eliciting a groan from the players.

"Craps is apparently bad," Darien said under her breath.

"It is unless you own the game."

She glanced at him. "Are you a big-time gambler?" she asked.

"If by big-time you mean win a lot, the answer is no."

"Do you lose a lot?"

"More than I win."

"You're being coy, Sam."

"I'm not a regular, but when I do gamble a few thousand is usually hanging in the balance."

Her eyes widened. "Really?"

"It's not a lot by Las Vegas standards, believe me."

"Do you play craps?"

"Some. Baccarat more than anything else."

"You're certainly dressed for it tonight," Darien said.

"Later, after the show, I thought I'd take you over to the MGM. They have a separate baccarat salon."

"Is that good?"

"If you prefer that the guy taking your money be in a tuxedo, it is."

She blinked. "You're an elitist, aren't you, Sam?"

He gave her an inquiring look, as if to ask if she really wished to know.

"No," she said, reading his thought, "that wasn't my second question. I was only curious what it meant."

"Well, I'm not an elitist. I just like dressing up. There aren't many opportunities the way people live nowadays. But lest you think I'm totally self-absorbed, you should know my annual donations to charity far exceed my self-indulgences."

"Is that supposed to reassure me?"

"Do you feel the need for reassurance, Darien?" His voice was low and surprisingly serious.

"I'd like to think you're a good guy...under that high-society veneer."

"If that's important to you, then so be it."

"Just like that?" she said incredulously.

"Darien, my dear, this weekend is about fantasy, not reality. You mustn't forget that." He took her arm. "Come on, let's have dinner. I'm beginning to get hungry."

As Sam guided her to the restaurant, she realized a pattern was beginning to form. He proposed, then she complied. He made a show of consideration, though he was clearly in charge. And she was incapable of doing anything about it. She wasn't even sure she wanted to.

The elaborate entry to the Ibis restaurant was guarded by six larger-than-life-size statues facing each other, like the guards to a royal tomb. But the interior of the restaurant was anything but funereal. The domed ceiling was midnight blue and covered with golden stars. The room was decorated in earth tones that were accented by the deep green of the plants. There were quite a few dramatic pieces of statuary enclosed in glass. Isis was in the center of the room, lit like a gleaming jewel. Other figures ringed the circular space.

Darien slipped into the booth and Sam sat next to her. The table was set with mosaic patterned service plates and oversize crystal. She took her napkin and looked across the table at him.

"Very elegant."

"I must say, you look like you belong here, Darien. The perfect accent to the room."

Her cheeks colored at the compliment, but she knew the dim light wouldn't allow him to see it. "Thank you."

Sam gave her a long, penetrating look. "Everything I've said, you know, is quite sincere."

"You're just falling into the role."

He shook his head. "If I'm guilty of anything, it's of allowing myself a few fantasies of my own."

The waiter arrived and they turned to their menus.

They dined on Caesar salad, pheasant and French champagne. The salad and the champagne were starting to be a ritual for them, but this time, Darien was careful not to drink too much. She needed a clear head.

Sam chose not to be provocative, instead engaging her in conversation. She told him some of the more important things about her life and work, though not about Todd. Sam's questions were thoughtful, and she had a feeling he really wanted to know the answers. She couldn't recall ever being with a man and being the topic of conversation to such a degree. She liked it.

Even so, after the waiter brought coffee she decided the time had come to bring the situation into perspective. "You know, Sam, anonymity is one thing, but it's not easy to relate to someone I know nothing about."

"You wish to relate to me."

"Yes. I'd feel more comfortable having a sense of who you are."

"You had a pretty clear concept of me in your article. I could relate to the man you described. And identify with him. That partly explains why I'm here. I *am* Sam."

"In other words, you don't want to tell me anything."

"All right, I'll do what I can to satisfy your desire to relate to me better." He paused to take a sip of coffee. "Like you, Sam's an only child. Father deceased, mother living. He's single, straight and has never been married. He's fully engaged in his career, but not obsessed. He likes to play. To amuse. To give pleasure."

"And he likes to titillate," she said. "Don't leave that one out."

"You think so?"

"You're a scoundrel, Sam."

"Well, maybe a little."

"How dangerous are you?"

"Now that depends on your frame of reference," he said.

She gave him a tight smile. "You know quite a bit about me. How dangerous are you from *my* frame of reference?"

"I'd have to say right on the borderline."

She blinked. "What does that mean?"

"We both know a certain amount of danger appeals to you," he said, "otherwise you wouldn't be here. Let's put it this way—I can probably give you all the danger you want . . . and then some."

"I bet you can. But that's not very reassuring."

"Ah. Apparently you don't leave your hand in the flame when it starts to burn."

"You got that right."

"Well, I know now not to burn you."

"You love these little mind games."

"No more than you, Darien."

She fiddled with her coffee cup. "You realize you aren't telling me a damned thing I don't already know."

"I'm thirty-six."

"And yet you've never been married. No close calls?"

"One or two. Nothing serious, though."

"You're basically a playboy, then."

"No. I haven't callously hurt anyone. Where possible, I've tried to spare feelings."

"But you've left a few women in tears."

"Possibly."

"No, Sam, most assuredly."

He sipped his coffee. "You consider that a black mark?"

"I'd have to know the circumstances, but it's easy to see how you could create expectations you had no intention of fulfilling."

"You think I use people?" he asked.

"Maybe not intentionally."

"Tell me, how does that fit in with your fantasy?"

"Oh, in my fantasies there's never a problem. I'm always master of my emotions."

"But you don't like it easy," he said. "There's no fun without a challenge."

"You think you've got me all figured out."

"I'm a careful reader, Darien, and your article revealed a great deal. At the risk of immodesty, you told me all I needed to know."

She nodded, her expression bemused. "Like most men who've been successful with the ladies, you're a smug SOB, aren't you?"

"Only to a point," he said. "But if I do misjudge, I'll rely on you to inform me."

"Oh, you don't have to worry about that, Sam," she said with a laugh.

"So you see, there's really nothing to fear. All you need to know is what you want."

Darien studied him. They maintained eye contact, staring each other down. Finally, after a long, long time, she gave in. "I've got an admission to make," she said. "I don't know whether to believe you or not. You could be giving me the best line in the history of western civilization and I wouldn't know the difference."

He shrugged. "Think of the fun you'll have finding out." He slid his hand over and affectionately touched hers. "So, what do you think, milady? Ready to go play?"

She engaged his eyes again. This time hers began to shimmer. "They say it's a mistake to expose your weaknesses in a negotiation," she said, "but I think I'll take the risk. Before we go I want to tell you something about my past that I left out earlier."

Sam leaned back. "Oh? Is this something a he?"

Darien nodded.

"He has a name, I assume."

"Yes, it's Todd," she said softly. "We were engaged, but shortly before the wedding he was killed in an accident."

"I'm sorry. Was this recent?"

"No, years ago." She fiddled absently with her bare ring finger. "The only reason I mention it is that it's probably the most formative experience in my adult life. And in an odd way, it might even explain why the notion of playing out a fantasy enticed me."

"It seemed safe," he said, clearly understanding.

"In an emotional sense, yes."

He drew his index finger over the back of her hand. "Don't worry," he said, his voice scarcely above a whisper, "I know how to be gentle."

A shiver went up and down her spine. Her heart gave a tiny lurch. His eyes glistened, the same as hers. She felt a well of gratitude and warmth. For some reason, she didn't believe his compassion could be anything but sincere. She still didn't know him, but she felt much better than only a few minutes before.

Reading her, he pulled her hand to his lips and kissed her fingers. Her eyes shimmered through a well of tears.

"I think we need a change of subject," he said, his voice low and mellow.

Darien wiped away the tear at the corner of her eye. "I'm sure you're right."

Sam checked his watch. "We have an hour and a half before the show. How about returning to the casino for some action?"

"Action, as in gambling?"

"Sure. You've got money burning a hole in your pocket...or, considering the way that dress fits you, your credit line. Might as well avail yourself."

"You'll have to teach me."

He gave her a broad smile—the same smile that had thawed her heart the first time she'd seen it. "That, my dear, is what fantasy men are for." He signaled the waiter.

Darien drew a breath, a confused jumble of emotions washing over her. He'd given her a glimpse of his humanity, of himself. Whether he'd done it with specific intent or not, the effect of it induced her to let down her guard. That might be naive, even foolish, but she sensed the die had been cast.

8

THEY STROLLED ABOUT, Darien with her hand in the crook of his arm. The mood in the casino was a curious combination of serious and exciting. Only the craps tables were raucous. The blackjack tables were more relaxed, but Darien was not drawn to them for some reason.

Sam guided her to a roulette table where there were only three players, a middle-aged Asian gentleman in a silk suit and dark-rimmed glasses, a shaggy-haired cowboy in jeans and a clean shirt and a woman who looked to be a forty-something school teacher. The Asian gentleman, whose much younger companion was dripping with jewelry, had an enormous pile of blue chips in front of him, yet he acted surprisingly indifferent, even unhappy. The teacher had half as many pale green chips, yet she appeared to be enjoying herself. The cowboy, whose chips were yellow, had somewhat fewer than the woman.

Darien and Sam watched them play. The Asian smiled mildly when he won, the other two were more demonstrative. Only the teacher watched the ball circle the wheel then bounce before landing in a numbered slot.

When Darien said she did not understand the placement of the chips on the board, Sam explained it was possible to bet on more than one number with the same chip, depending on the way it was placed on the layout.

"For example, if you place a chip on the intersection where four numbers touch, you're betting on all four. It's called a square and it pays eight to one odds instead of thirty-five to one, if you were betting on a single number. You can bet on two numbers at a time, a whole row of numbers, a column, odd numbers, even numbers, black or red and other combinations. The odds vary depending on the bet."

"The odds must not be very good," she said.

"Oh, they're mathematically fair, except for the fact that there are two extra slots on the wheel, the zero and the double zero. Over the long run that gives the house a five percent advantage. The result is that players will eventually lose."

"Then why do people play?" she asked.

"Because they believe in luck." He chuckled. "They also plan to quit when they're ahead, but they seldom do."

Darien couldn't tell if the far-off look in his eye related to a gambling memory or to something else. "Do you quit when you're ahead?" she asked.

"Sometimes I do and sometimes I don't."

She decided to try a different way. "Are you lucky?" she asked.

He grinned.

She knew what he was going to say. "Sometimes you are and sometimes you aren't, right?"

He nodded. "So, how about you? Want to try your luck?"

While she considered the question, he made the decision for her by signaling the pit boss to come over.

"Ms. Hughes would like five hundred dollars to play some roulette," he said.

"Five hundred?" Darien said.

"Would you like more?"

"Twenty dollars would seem extravagant to me," she said.

The men exchanged smiles.

"Make it four hundred," Sam said.

The pit boss asked to see the identity card Darien had been given when she checked in. Then he had her sign a receipt and asked the dealer to give her four one-hundred-dollar chips.

"You can use them to buy a color," Sam explained. "Pick any that's not in use."

Darien considered the options. "I guess I'll take rose," she said.

"Good choice," Sam said into her ear. "Goes well with your dress."

She nudged him with her elbow. "Are you being snide?"

"No, I'm getting good vibrations. I have a feeling you'll be lucky." He squeezed her waist. Darien liked the feel of him touching her. It felt right. Sam gestured for her to sit on the stool in front of them.

"How many dollar chips, miss?" the dealer asked as the ball spun counterclockwise in the wheel.

Darien looked at the four chips in her hand, thinking each of them represented a lot of groceries. "One hundred," she said, putting a chip on the table.

"One hundred," he repeated as he began to get the dollar chips.

The ivory ball had fallen into a slot meanwhile. The two dealers cleared the table and paid the winning bets. While the croupier stacked chips, the wheel roller pushed four stacks of rose-colored chips across the table in front of Darien.

"Place your bets, ladies and gentlemen," the dealer said as he spun the ball in the wheel. "Place your bets."

The other players were already hard at work covering the layout with chips. Darien looked at Sam. "You're going to have to help me," she said.

"You can start out slow," he said. "Take four chips and put them on red or black, odd or even."

"Why four?"

"That's the minimum on even money or two-to-one bets."

Darien put four chips on red. The other players had finished putting down their chips and the dealer announced there would be no more bets. A moment later the ball fell from the track, bounced around the wheel a few times and landed in the five slot. Darien saw that the five was a red number. She looked up at Sam, smiling.

"You're a winner," he said. "You just made four bucks."

She watched the dealer put four rose-colored chips from his reserve next to the ones she'd bet.

"Do I take them?" she asked Sam.

"Unless you want to let them ride."

She considered the matter. "It'll be red again."

"Maybe you'd like to add a few, if you're so sure," he said wryly.

"No, I'm happy with eight. But I want to bet on twenty-one, too."

"Your age?"

She gave him a look. "Don't be sarcastic."

"I thought I was being gallant," he said, feigning hurt feelings.

"If I'd said I wanted to bet on twenty-eight, I might have believed you." She reached across the table and put one of her chips on twenty-one, then waited for the ball to drop.

"Thirty-two," the dealer said. "Red thirty-two."

"I guessed wrong," she groused. "I was sure it was going to be twenty-one."

"But you won eight more dollars on red," Sam said.

Darien did a quick calculation. "Then I'm eleven dollars ahead."

"I bet that's the easiest eleven you ever made."

"It was."

Sam put his hand on the back of her neck where a few tendrils of hair had escaped. His touch sent shivers up and down her spine.

"Is it going to be red again?"

She shook her head. "I don't think so."

"Better pick up your chips, then."

She pulled the stacks toward her and the ball was spun.

"Place your bets, ladies and gentleman," the dealer said. "Place your bets."

Darien started to put four dollars on odd, then changed her mind. "What happens if it's zero or double zero?" she asked. "I'm almost sure it will hit one of those this time."

"Then you better put money on it."

She took two chips from her stack. Sam took them and put them on the line between the zero and the double zero.

"No more bets," the dealer intoned.

The ball bounced around and ended up on the double zero.

"Hey, you *are* lucky," Sam said as Darien clapped gleefully.

She looked around the table. The other players were not so pleased. The cowboy was down to his last few chips. The schoolteacher was about the same as before.

The Asian had gone down a little from when they'd arrived. On this play Darien was the only winner.

Two tall stacks of rose chips were pushed in front of her. Sam kept on caressing the back of her neck. Despite her excitement about winning, she was acutely aware of his touch.

"How many did I get?"

"Has to be over thirty," he said. "Let's see. Two on a split . . . that's a thirty-four, isn't it?" he asked the dealer.

"Yes, sir."

"That means I'm up forty-three dollars!" she said.

"Sounds to me like you're hooked," he said.

"No, I'll quit ahead, even if it's only a dollar."

When he chuckled, she elbowed him in the side. "You'll see, wise guy."

An hour later Darien was three hundred dollars to the good. At that point she decided to call it quits. Sam, who'd played and lost a couple of hundred dollars, watched with her as the dealers cashed them out. Most of the players were new. Only the Asian was still there from the original group. He'd gone through a thousand dollars by Darien's reckoning. She put the chips in her purse. Sam tipped the dealers ten dollars and they left.

"I have to admit that was fun," she said. "But I'm really not hooked. I can gamble for five years on what I made tonight, although in fairness my winnings really belong to you."

"Nonsense. Besides, I got my reward by watching you have a good time. If you want to know the truth, this was the most fun I've had gambling in years." He checked his watch. "We have a bit more time before the show begins. Would you like to have a drink?"

Darien shook her head. "I don't think so, Sam. Maybe we could just walk around. This has been a wonderful experience," she said as they strolled through the lobby. "You've gone way beyond the call of duty."

"We're just getting started."

He said it easily, without innuendo, but Darien read more into the comment, whether he intended it or not. Though he'd been a gentleman—albeit one walking the narrow line—how could he not have planned for them to end the evening in bed?

She had a veto power, of course. She could stop this thing right now, if she chose. But she had no desire to, at least not yet. She was letting things drift along without knowing what she really wanted, or when or how she'd decide.

If she did end up in bed with him, why had she picked Sam out of all of the men she'd met? And why now?

Since Todd had died she'd dated quite a few men, and she'd slept with some of them. But none had ever done much for her. Darien had never been sure if that was because of her, or because of them.

Sam was different. But even though she was certain of that, she wasn't sure exactly what it was about him that called to her. Maybe it was something as simple as the unreality of it all. Or perhaps it was because she didn't know the man behind the fantasy…and probably never would. In an odd sort of way that kept her from having any serious expectations. Yes. That must be what it was. Sam was emotionally safe because of his anonymity.

They had come to the boarding area for the guided boat trek down the Nile. It was late enough that the others waiting were couples only—two other couples beside themselves. They grabbed the seat at the rear of the boat. Sam slipped his arm around her shoulder and they were under way.

Darien found it easy to relax. He was comfortable to be with. Everything felt completely natural.

The boat drifted along as the quippy guide entertained them with information and anecdotes about ancient Egypt. Darien gazed at the soaring atrium and let herself get lost in the moment. Soon the sound of the guide's voice seemed to fade and the only thing she was aware of was Sam. She felt the heat of his body, the lime tang of his after-shave. He seemed warm and solid, even if he continued to elicit feelings of doubt and apprehension. Surprisingly, the danger he represented was starting to be more positive than negative. She was getting hooked.

Sam was so perfectly suited for the role of seducer. Not only was he physically attractive and likable, but he had the willingness, the imagination and resources to play this exotic game of titillation with her, and to make her crave more.

"You're being rather quiet," Sam said softly into her ear. "Is all that thinking you're doing a good omen or ill?"

"Good for whom?" she said, giving him an ironic smile.

"Me. I might as well be blatantly egocentric."

"I admire your candor."

"If a person is going to play night games, a certain amount of honesty is necessary."

"So that's what this is, a night game."

He shrugged. "For want of a better term. Yes."

She took a deep breath. "Well, at least we're on the same page now. I know where I stand."

"And is that okay with you?"

"I don't know why, but yes. It is. Besides, my readers didn't expect me to come down here to play miniature golf."

"You're beginning to trust me," he said, running his index finger along the edge of her jaw.

His touch made her shiver. "I hope the trust is warranted."

He pressed his lips softly against her ear. "I've already promised to be gentle," he whispered.

Another tremor went through her. She considered, but decided against, asking him to elaborate. Instead she eased her body against him, putting her hand on his thigh. Sam took the exchange as a signal. And it had been. She'd let him know she was willing, because she didn't want to drag out the tension. If they were going to play night games, there was no reason to be coy. After all, she was a big girl now.

DARIEN NEVER drank martinis, though in college Julie Bellingham had once told her that they were the closest thing to an aphrodisiac she'd found. Darien had argued that sexual desire came from the mind, not a bottle, but Julie swore that martinis never failed to put her in a sexy mood.

Darien didn't consider that she was in need of help in that regard, but when they'd been seated at ringside in the Pharaoh's Dinner Theater, and the waiter came for their drink orders, she unhesitatingly asked for a martini. Sam ordered Scotch and held her hand, playing with her fingers while they waited for their drinks.

When he squeezed her fingers she looked into his eyes. "Has this gone pretty much as you expected?" she asked.

"Why do you ask?"

"Curiosity. You obviously have everything carefully choreographed." When a momentary look of distress crossed his face, she quickly added, "To quote you earlier, that wasn't meant as a criticism, just an observation."

"I believe every date, every relationship has to be played by ear," he said. "I didn't expect this evening to go badly, by any means, but I recognized it was possible. I'd like to think the reason it's going well, Darien, is that we both want it to."

She sighed. He seemed to be ready with the right thing to say no matter what came up, no matter what sort of curve she threw. Sam was refusing to disappoint her, even as he insisted on bedeviling her.

Their drinks were served. After they touched glasses, she took a healthy slug of her martini, silently saluting her friend Julie. It was nearly time for the show to begin, and the last of the spectators were being seated. Soon, the lights began to fade. Sam let go of her hand and the show began.

Over an hour later, after witnessing an epic tale of good versus evil complete with beautiful, scantily clad women, muscular men and all the promised excitement and spectacle, they left the theater. Sam slipped his arm around her waist.

"Was it worth the plane ride?" he asked.

"Everything has been wonderful. More than I had a right to expect." She'd had two martinis and was beginning to think maybe Julie was onto something, though reason told her the origins of her feelings were in her head.

"What's your pleasure now, milady?" he asked. "If you want to experience a baccarat salon we can go over to the MGM. It's only a block away. The air is probably nice out. We can walk, if that appeals to you."

"If it's important to you, I'll go," she said, "but don't do it for me. I'd be content to step outside for some air."

"Let's go out by the pool, then, and see if there's a moon."

Darien liked the idea. "All right."

They'd made their way up to the casino level with the rest of the show crowd, and taking her hand, Sam led the way to the doors leading outside. She'd gone by the pool on the way to the spa that afternoon, but at night the feel was completely different.

As they strolled around the huge pool across the lawn, Darien looked at the pyramid. Sure enough, there was a moon coming up behind the huge black building. "It's not Egypt, and it's not a crescent moon, but it's pretty," she said.

"Yes, and so are you."

She turned to him. In the moonlight Sam was dramatically handsome. The deep shadow and cool glow of the muted light enhanced the effect. He was looking at her as if he wanted to kiss her. He put his hands on her waist, and she again felt the warmth of his palms through the silk. But this time she was more receptive and far less uncertain.

He drew her closer and lowered his mouth toward hers. Their lips brushed. His felt moist and soft. When his mouth covered hers, he pulled her more firmly against him. Darien was filled with a strong and immediate desire. Her heart beat more swiftly and she felt her nipples grow taut.

When their lips finally parted, Sam held her as if he didn't have the slightest intention of ever letting her go. Darien peered over his shoulder at the night sky, trying to catch her breath. Her heart was pounding so hard she thought he surely must feel it. She was aware of his fingers on her bare back, the comfortable fit of their bodies.

"Those martinis must have been stronger than I thought," she murmured.

"I hope you aren't going to give all the credit to them."

She pulled back so that she could see his face, touching his chin with her fingertip. "You may have had something to do with it."

Sam smiled. Then he kissed her lightly, keeping the caress tender and loving. She felt her body begin to tingle. Maybe it was from long months of abstinence, or maybe it was just Sam, or maybe Julie was right about the martinis, after all. Whatever the explanation, Darien knew she wanted to go to bed with him.

He was kissing the side of her neck, arousing her still more, washing his breath over her tingling skin.

"Sam," she whispered, "I want you to take me to my room now. And I want you to stay."

He stopped kissing. There was a glint of satisfaction in his eyes but he said nothing.

"Maybe it's what I've wanted all along," she said, "since the day you came to the paper to see me."

"It's what I've wanted since that day," he replied. "Though I've tried not to be too obvious."

"Was it me, or what I'd written?"

"Both," he said, lightly kissing her lips. "In case I haven't mentioned this before, you appeal equally to my body *and* my mind. You had me seduced from almost the moment I saw you."

"And so you concocted this elaborate game in order to get me into bed?"

He traced her lower lip with his finger. "I'd say it was a mutual effort. A man can't do much more than propose a relationship," he said.

Darien kissed his finger. "He can make it damned near impossible to say no."

There was a twinge of a smile on his lips. "May the result be as gratifying as the promise." Then, holding her tight, he whispered, "Come play with me, Darien. It's time."

9

SAM OPENED the door to Darien's suite, they went inside, and then he carefully closed the door behind them. He joined her in the sitting room and casually took her hand.

"Would you like a drink?" she asked.

He shook his head. "I don't care for one, but I'll fix you something, if you like."

Darien moved close enough to touch him, to feel the warmth of his body. She fingered the studs on his dress shirt, running her nail under the edge of the pleats. "Maybe I'll have another martini, if you can fix one," she said without looking up at him.

"If there's vodka, I can fix a very dry one," he teased.

She acknowledged his comment with a smile, then peered into his eyes, wanting to feel good about the way things were headed. But she already felt the first hints of self-doubt creeping in. Sam didn't move.

"What?" she said, uncertain what he was thinking.

"Somehow you don't seem like a martini drinker to me," he said.

"I'm not, normally."

"Dutch courage?" he said.

"It wouldn't be very flattering if I needed courage to be with you, now would it?"

"No, but the truth is the truth."

"I'm a little frightened," she confessed. "It's not easy going to bed with a man whose name I don't even know.

You could be a charlatan and a fraud. For all I know you've filled my ears with honey and lies just so you can use me for your own immoral purposes."

He grinned. "Is that intended as a suggestion . . . or a complaint?"

"Oh, Sam! You know what I mean. I may not be up to this game."

"We can reverse gears."

She set her hand flat on his pleated chest. "No, that's not what I'm saying."

"Then what are you saying?"

She took a few deep breaths and shifted uncomfortably. "Convince me, Sam."

He looked hard into her eyes but held his tongue. It was difficult to tell if he was amused by her trepidation or annoyed. She felt so stupid and yet so needy, so childlike and yet so wanton.

He ran his fingertips over her bare shoulders. She inhaled his musky scent, wanting to experience him still more intimately. He leaned over and kissed her shoulders, her collarbone. When her head rolled back he kissed her neck, pressing his moist lips against her skin.

Darien's knees felt weak, and her balance grew unsteady. She moaned, the pleasure of his touch igniting her desire. He held her by the waist, his fingers pressing the silk of the gown into her flesh. Her heart stuttered. His mouth found hers and they kissed deeply.

After the kiss ended he held her tightly. She could hear his ragged breathing and feel his chest rise against her breast. "Still want that drink?" he asked.

Darien shook her head. "No, but I do want to freshen up. I'll meet you in the bedroom." She slipped from his arms, hurrying through the bedroom to the bath.

The face waiting for her in the bathroom mirror was flushed, her cheeks glowing, her breathing heavy and uneven. She'd wanted him to arouse her, and he had done that and more. She felt like someone doing her best to compromise her virtue, running headlong toward trouble while knowing her impulsiveness was foolish. It was almost as though she had some sort of death wish.

Darien dabbed her cheeks with a damp cloth, anxiously searching her heart and mind for guidance. A few hours earlier she had stood in that very spot visiting the past—Julie, Carter, Ryan, the lawyer Julie had wanted to set her up with. And of course, she'd thought of Todd. Even in death he'd continued to be a factor, influencing her life the way background music affected the mood of an occasion.

But the past was dead now, even if it wasn't forgotten. Years had passed. She was thirty, living her own life and making her own decisions. One of them had been to come to Las Vegas for an exciting sexy weekend with the man of her fantasies. She'd made that decision for one simple reason—the man she loved was no more.

Her eyes turned glossy and began to brim. She told herself there was no reason to cry. If tears could solve her problem they'd have done it years ago. The only thing to do now was get on with her life. And that wasn't such a terrible fate.

Sam had aroused her from her lethargy, fired her physically and emotionally. True, he wasn't Todd. But in an odd way she was no longer the Darien Hughes who had loved and lost so many years ago, either. She'd grown and changed and grown some more. For the first time in her life she was accepting her sexuality, defining her needs and desires in terms of what would please her.

No doubt about it, Sam was the physical embodiment of her dreams. She'd taken one long, languorous look at him that day on the deck at Sam's and she'd wanted him. She hadn't even stopped to ask herself what he was really like. Instead, she'd filled in the shadows of his personality with traits and characteristics that would appeal to her, meet her needs. And the real man, the flesh and blood Sam waiting for her in the other room, had not been a disappointment. He *was* Sam. For the first time in years the brass ring was hers for the taking. All she had to do now was reach out and grab it.

Tucking a tendril into her hair, she left the bath. Sam was waiting in the bedroom. The only light in the room came from the lamp by the window. He sat on the bed, a martini in his hand. He'd removed his jacket. Darien didn't know why men in a formal dress shirt, cummerbund and bow tie always looked half naked without their jacket, but they did. Half naked and sexy.

"I made you a drink anyway," he said, holding it out for her. "Just in case I'm too much for you sober."

She walked over to him and put her hand on his shoulder. "Don't think that way, Sam. The problem is you're too enticing."

She took the proffered glass anyway and gulped down some of the liquid. The alcohol stung her throat. Her eyes teared. Sam looked as if he wasn't sure what to make of her behavior. His expression was vaguely melancholy.

"You make a good martini," she said.

"I guess I can take it as a compliment, even though you never drink them."

"I don't run around kissing men all the time, but with some assurance I can still say you kiss well."

"I take your point." His tone of voice was thoughtful, not exactly sorrowful but cheerless.

When he reached out and took her left hand to play with her ring finger, she understood why. He was wondering what kind of ring she had worn on it once upon a time.

"It was a two-carat diamond," she murmured. "When he gave it to me, I thought it was the most wonderful ring on earth."

"Do you still have it?"

"Yes, but I never wear it. Frankly I'm not sure what to do with it. There weren't any children to pass it on to, of course. What does one do with a ring from a deceased fiancé?"

Sam continued to caress her finger, but didn't answer.

"His family didn't want it back." She took one more sip of the martini, then put the glass on the shelf in the alcove above the headboard. She'd had enough. More would not be good.

Behind her, she heard Sam rise from the bed. The next thing she knew his hands were on her shoulders and he was kissing the back of her neck. Why she'd been so stupid as to talk about Todd she'd never know. Poor Sam. Her would-be husband had to be the last person on earth he cared to hear about just then.

But when Sam drew the tip of his tongue up the side of her neck, she forgot about Todd. She forgot about everything except the feel of Sam's touch. When he slid his hands down her arms and cupped her breasts she moaned, letting her head roll back.

Sam nibbled his way up her neck to her ear. At the same time his thumbs stroked her nipples through the silk of the dress. She let out a tiny groan of pleasure.

Turning abruptly in his arms to face him, Darien covered his mouth with hers, biting at his lips. She wanted to provoke him, to take as well as be taken, to give as well as get. Their tongues entwined and she opened her mouth a bit wider.

When their long kiss finally ended, she pulled away to look into Sam's eyes. They were dark—not just the deep blue she'd gotten used to, but dark with passion. And the yearning she saw reflected in them mirrored her own feelings.

Never before had she felt such a desire to give herself up completely to the emotion of the moment. All she wanted was to feel. And the feeling she wanted above all others was that of Sam making love to her.

"I don't want to wait any longer," she murmured. "Please make love to me."

He didn't rush. He kissed her once more, slowly. Then he moved his hand to the back of her dress and unzipped it. Darien let the gown slither to the floor. She stepped out of it, then, with more courage than she knew she had, she took off her panty hose and bikini panties.

Sam watched as she stripped. He didn't smile or leer or offer to help. It was as if he knew she wanted to do this alone. Perhaps he even sensed that she was proving something to herself—something he'd probably never understand. Yet it was a form of understanding that he recognized her need and accepted it.

Sam stepped over to the chair by the window then and began undressing. When he was naked he turned to her. He was tall and lean, well-formed and muscular. And he didn't seem the least bit embarrassed that she stared at him.

"Do you want the light on or off?"

"I want it on," she said simply. He did smile then, as if he was pleased that she didn't want to hide what they were going to do.

Darien stepped into his arms. He felt warm and alive. She ran her hand over his chest, marveling that the mat of hair was silky rather than crinkly. It felt good. Being in his arms was even better than looking at him. He seemed to be muscle and bone and flesh, smooth and hard, all at the same time.

"I like your body," she said. Then she buried her face in his chest, embarrassed that she'd spoken so forthrightly.

Sam rubbed the back of her neck with one hand and pressed his other hand against her derriere, pulling her so close that she felt the bulge between his legs.

"I'm glad."

There were to be no professions of love, Darien knew that. This was to be a sexual ritual, aimed at gratification, pure and simple. Sam would take what she had to give, and in so doing give something back to her.

She pulled away so she could look into his eyes, wanting to know the source of her pleasure as best she could. "There are a lot of questions I should probably ask before doing this. And you, too, for that matter."

"I know."

"You don't have to give me your sexual history, Sam, but I'd appreciate knowing whether I'll be safe. That can be my second question for the day."

"You'll be safe," he said. "And I won't charge you for the answer. That much you're entitled to know."

He drew his hand up her thigh and her side, then slid it around her back, running his thumb up and down her spine. She felt his firmness as he squeezed her against him. The intimacy sent a tremor through her.

"Do you like it slow and gentle or do you prefer it more forceful?" he asked, speaking through his teeth.

He was as aroused as she. His hunger was a bit frightening.

"Don't hurt me," she murmured. "Otherwise, do what you want."

He sank his fingers into her flesh, sending a surge of excitement and apprehension through her. "You like it all, then?"

His tone was cold and wanton, sexually threatening. In spite of that it turned her on.

"Everything," she said. Her voice sounded small and tentative, even to her.

With that he swept her into his arms and walked the couple of feet over to the bed. He set her down across the foot of it, but before she could even squirm around to right herself he bent over and began kissing her.

She responded at once, glad that the talking was over. This was what she'd wanted—to be naked in his arms. Thankfully, he seemed to understand her need. Sam kissed and caressed, used his hands and mouth to arouse her, play with her, make her feel strange new sensations and familiar old ones. He led her down a path where the only thing that mattered was pleasure—a kind of pleasure she didn't think existed except in fantasies.

She was feeling warm and relaxed and wet when Sam suddenly slid off the bed and knelt at the edge of it. To her surprise, he began kissing her toes. At first it tickled and she tried to pull away. But when it started turning her on, she lay quietly, staring at the ceiling. She wondered why on earth she'd never before thought of feet as being sensuous. They were. Oh, yes, they definitely were.

Sam licked and sucked and kissed each toe before dragging his tongue over her instep to her knee. He stopped there, just when she was sure he meant to keep on going, and started the process over again, with the other foot.

Within minutes Darien was on the edge. She was very wet and hot and she shivered when he blew on the moist patches where his tongue had swept over her skin. A part of her wanted him to stop teasing. An even bigger part of her loved the torment and wanted it to go on forever.

After what seemed like an eternity, Sam began nibbling up the inside of her thighs. The closer he got to the juncture of her legs, the more excited she got. When he finally reached her nub she jerked violently. He pleasured her with feathery swishes of his tongue, and it was all she could do to keep from crying out. But Darien didn't want it to end that way. For some reason she didn't quite understand, she knew it was important that he be inside her first, that she be a part of him.

She was at the point where she knew she couldn't hold off any longer when Sam climbed over her. Her legs were spread wide, and he was poised over her, looking into her eyes. Darien gazed at him, seeing passion but also distance, animal lust.

She placed her hands on his buttocks to indicate that she wanted him in her. Sam touched her with the tip of his penis. She cocked her hips, trying to take him in, but he only went in an inch or so before withdrawing. Then he did the same thing again and again, teasing her until she was wild with wanting him.

Finally, when she was literally clawing his back, he plunged all the way into her. For a moment it seemed as if it would be too much. But soon she found herself moving with him, wanting and taking more with each thrust.

She was sure they could go on like this forever. She never wanted it to end. But all too soon he had her back on the edge, nearing climax. This time she couldn't hold off. "Oh, now, Sam, please. Now."

With that, he plunged into her a final time and they both came. Afterward he collapsed onto her. They stayed like that for a long time, neither speaking. Sam roused himself enough to kiss her forehead, then her cheek before he rolled to the side, taking her with him so that they were still fused. His hand absently rubbed her back, caressing her, loving her. Darien had never felt so complete in her life, not physically.

"Is it always like that?" she asked. "Or was that special?"

"Each time is special. You're special."

"Oh. I just made love with a diplomat."

"Our chemistry is unusually good," he said softly, kissing the corner of her mouth.

"You don't have to try to make me feel good," she said. "It was great sex. Let's leave it at that."

"It isn't good unless you feel good about it afterward."

"I'm blissful, believe me. You're a hell of a lover, Sam. Better than I imagined."

Sam came out of her then and settled onto his back, sighing. "You aren't the only one who enjoyed that," he said.

Darien snuggled up to him, wanting to pretend the affection was meaningful. The warmth of his body was wonderful. Now that they were no longer making love, the air-conditioning made the room seem a little bit cool.

"Do you want to get under the covers?" he said.

Darien nodded. They both got up so they could pull down the bedding. As soon as Darien got under the covers she scooted close to him. The light by the window was still on, but it was behind her, so she was able to see his face, though it was partly shadowed. He looked handsome as ever, yet different somehow.

"What are you thinking?" he asked.

She sighed. "That you seem . . . I don't know, different, maybe. Now that we've made love, I mean."

"I am different, Darien. So are you. We're a part of each other's memories and nothing will change that."

She shivered. "You make love *and* you do poetry."

"Don't belittle it," he said. "That was a beautiful experience."

"But transitory. Let's don't make it something it wasn't."

"You're being defensive again."

"Am I?" she said.

He kissed her temple. "You're a beautiful woman, a fabulous lover, an exciting, stimulating companion."

"And *you're* trying to make me feel all right about having had anonymous sex."

"It wasn't anonymous."

"You use your term, I'll use mine."

"Whether you like it or not, we'll always have tonight."

"You make it sound permanent."

"It is permanent. At least, as long as our memories hold out." He leaned over and kissed her lips. "But just in case that wasn't enough for you to remember me by, maybe I ought to make sure you have something else to recall."

He started caressing her again, playing with her curls for a moment before he dipped a finger inside her. This time he moved more slowly, taking his time, savoring the experience. He licked and sucked her nipples until they were hard as pebbles. And when she told him she was

ready he turned her onto her stomach and took her from
behind.

He did everything he could to prolong her orgasm, re-
peatedly bringing her to the brink of climax before stopping. Then, when she was no longer on the edge, he'd
begin again, repeating the pattern. Finally, neither of
them could wait any longer.

It was a long time before either of them moved after
that. Darien could feel herself pulsing for several minutes. Every part of her seemed alive, extra sensitive.

They made love the last time just before dawn. Sam
awoke her with a kiss. But that time Darien wanted to
give back some of the joy he'd given her. She began by
kissing his neck all the way to his waist. Her tongue cir-
cled his navel and then moved lower. She kissed his penis.

Sam protested that it was her fantasy, that he should
be the one giving her pleasure. But when she took him
into her mouth he stopped talking. He was hard almost
at once. Darien straddled him and they made love that
way. And when he rolled her onto her back she wrapped
her legs around him and he took her beautifully.

Darien stayed awake for a long time after Sam went to
sleep, thinking about what she'd done. Never before had
sex been so thrilling. Never before had she felt so fulfilled. And she thought how strange that was.

She had loved Todd, truly loved him. Sex with him
had been exciting, yet it had lacked the passion she had
just experienced. She and Sam had shared something el-
emental, maybe because the sex was just that—sex for
the sake of having sex. Personalities hadn't come into
play. In a way, she thought, this was probably what it
was like when a man paid for a woman's body. And yet
she knew that analogy wasn't quite right, either.

True, she didn't know Sam. But she did know quite a bit about the kind of person he was. She was sure he was basically decent, kind and generous. He had a fine mind, a good sense of humor. He liked to play games but he had a serious side, too. She'd seen a thoughtfulness and consideration in him that was so often lacking in the guys she'd met since Todd died. Yet that didn't explain it, either. She fell asleep, still not sure what it was that made him so special. Perhaps in the morning she'd find out.

10

THE LIMOUSINE came around the curve on the James Lick Freeway, bringing the nighttime skyline of San Francisco into view. Darien hadn't been a resident of the city long enough to experience the feeling of deep familiarity upon returning home that she would have liked, but seeing the city did give her a sense of being back in the real world.

Of course, Sam had been real enough the night before. But the farther she got from Las Vegas, the more unreal the experience had become in her memory. When she'd awakened late that morning he was already gone. He'd disappeared without a sign, without a word of goodbye, not even a note. If his scent hadn't lingered in the pillow, she'd have had no proof he'd even been there.

She was a bit miffed at first because some parting word seemed the minimum he could do. But when she thought about it, who was she to complain? She'd used him for her own pleasure. And at his expense. Still, it would have been nice if there'd been a gracious denouement, a friendly, dignified end to the adventure.

Well, it was over now, and there was no denying her sexual escapade had been fabulous, even better than in her fantasies, because she hadn't known that kind of pleasure existed. She was grateful for that. The next step was to move on, put Sam behind her once and for all.

She suspected that wouldn't be easy. In a lot of ways the man was like chocolate—she'd wanted to satiate herself on him, and she had. But the memory of being with him remained sweet and enticing. She craved more. Maybe that's what Sam had intended all along—his ultimate victory. After all, every game had its winner and its loser.

In a moment of paranoia, she'd even wondered if he'd had something to hide. For all she knew, he could be a criminal, or married. When she'd checked out of the hotel that morning she'd asked where the bill was being sent. The clerk claimed he didn't know since the account had been handled by higher management. Annoyed, she'd asked to speak with the manager, who would only say that the bill had been settled anonymously. Darien realized then that there was no point in pressing matters further.

Before she knew it, the limo turned onto her street and she was stepping out into a light fog. The driver took her suitcase from the trunk and set it just inside the gate. She handed him a couple of dollars, grabbed her case and headed wearily toward her cottage.

Passing the main house, she could hear Dean and Marc talking inside. Judging by the sound of their voices, they were having a disagreement about something. Affectionate bickering seemed to be their way of relating to each other.

Once inside the cottage, Darien plopped down in a chair and listened to the silence—the yawning emptiness that symbolized her single life. In truth, though, she'd never lived completely alone—she'd always had memories of Todd. In that sense she'd been more like a widow.

But something had happened in Las Vegas that changed things. Sam had sparked something inside her, aroused a sleeping monster she hadn't known existed.

Neither the past nor the future would ever be the same. Somehow, she would have to deal with that.

DARIEN'S ARTICLE on her trip to Las Vegas became the talk of the town. People everywhere debated whether her account was fact or fiction. Even her closest colleagues weren't quite sure, but there was no doubt that she'd managed to be provocative... again.

The afternoon the article appeared, Rod Barker came by her cubicle with a copy of the paper in his hand. Pulling a straight chair over, he sat facing her, and leaning close, he said, "Just between us chickens, Hughes, none of this happened, right? You were the one who paid the guy to come here in the Egyptian suit. Sam's just fiction, am I right?"

"Rod," Darien replied in an equally conspiratorial tone, "Sam's as real as you want him to be. I'll leave it at that."

The sportswriter did not like her response. "Why be coy? We're both professionals here."

"Professionals respect one another's professionalism," she said. "I wish you'd respect mine."

Rod got to his feet and tossed the paper on the chair. "Pretty damned convenient that the guy disappears into thin air, never to be seen again, isn't it?" With that he walked out.

Darien absently picked up the newspaper Rod had left. It was folded to the page where her article appeared. She began reading near the end. When she'd written the words, she'd written them to the guy in Las Vegas she knew as Sam.

Sam had proved to me that fantasies can come true. But I learned another, perhaps more important lesson, as well. In many ways life is just a game—or, more accurately, a series of games. We dress up, we have our fun, we play until time runs out, but we don't take it too seriously. The next day the game might well be a different one with new rules, new objectives, new players. The reality is that there are some things in life we simply can't control. And so we learn to accept whatever fate brings to our door, and go on.

I will always remember my weekend in Las Vegas with Sam. He taught me about pleasure, but whether he intended it or not, he also taught me something important about myself. For that I will always be grateful.

Shortly before Darien left for the evening, Bob Smits called her into his office.

"Another fine piece of writing," he said, "but frankly, I don't know whether to laugh or cry."

"As long as you're moved by it, that's all that matters," she said. "Right?"

"I wasn't referring to the substance of the article so much as the implications. Is it my imagination, or is Sam a thing of the past? Was this the last in the series?"

"I think so, Bob. Even if I hear from Sam again, which is doubtful, I'm not sure I want to do another one."

"Why?"

She sighed wearily. "I'm not sure I have any more to say on that topic. I was taught the time to quit a subject was before you had to start stretching to fill the space. I think Sam has run his course. Besides, I'm tired."

Bob had a long face and didn't say anything.

"Is that a problem?" she asked.

"The publicity department had a long chat with me this afternoon at Roger Gilbert's request. They've been getting some flack on your series. Even here there are prudes who'll take offense at anything, and the suggestion that you might have had a sexual relationship with Sam brought a flurry of cancellations, a few dozen."

"Then it's just as well I quit before it gets worse."

"That was the bad news. The good news is that there have been over fifteen hundred new subscriptions. They attribute ninety percent of them to your series. Roger is ecstatic."

Darien digested the implications. "I suppose he wouldn't be pleased if I stopped."

"It's never bad to make hay while the sun is shining, if you get my drift."

"You're saying I should milk it for all it's worth."

"You got to be true to yourself, but if you can find one or two more pieces in you, it'd make a lot of folks happy, including thousands of readers."

"I hate that kind of pressure, especially when it flies in the face of what I believe."

"Just keep an open mind. Don't bury Sam just yet."

She got up to leave.

"Oh, by the way, Mr. Gilbert authorized me to bump your salary a couple of hundred a week. I hope that pleases you."

"Yes, Bob, but it also makes me feel guilty as hell."

"Well, don't feel bad. Sam's not the only topic you can write about. You've got a following now. Take advantage of it."

Darien nodded and left his office. At her cubicle she gathered her things to head for home, suddenly feeling depressed. She'd rationalized the end of her relationship with Sam, but what she hadn't accounted for was a journalistic future without him. It was as if she had to go out and find a new fantasy lover, and that wasn't what she wanted. Sam was as good as it could possibly get.

DARIEN DIDN'T FEEL the least bit creative the next day. She called to say she wouldn't be coming in. She spoke to Virginia.

"I'll let Bob know," the receptionist said. "He won't care, I'm sure. You worked all weekend!" She laughed. "Good work, if you can get it, huh?"

"Yeah, great work."

Virginia sighed. "I don't mean to pry, but was he really wonderful? I mean, did he know his way around a woman's body?"

"Yes, I think you could safely say he did. I don't know if world class is an official designation for that sort of thing," Darien said, "but in my limited experience, I'd say he qualifies."

"Oh, to have been a fly on the wall."

"No, it's better to use your imagination. That's what good writing is supposed to do."

"You sure sparked me."

"Great."

"And I'm not the only one," Virginia said, popping her gum. "You won't believe the calls. Mostly it's women begging you not to dump Sam. I guess they're afraid it'll ruin their fantasy life. And there have been a few men who've called offering to take up where Sam left off."

"Well, I can't live my life for other people."

"Maybe you ought to make the stuff up, then. I know I don't care if it's true."

"Thanks for the suggestion, Virginia. I'll give it some thought."

"Got to run, the board's lighting up like a Christmas tree."

Darien hung up and went to make herself some coffee. She'd slept in, having awakened several times during the night. It had been like that since her return from Vegas. The memories of that night had stuck with her. No, they obsessed her. Bedeviled her. All she could think of was the pleasure. Sam had really put her in touch with her sexuality. She hadn't realized how stifled and repressed she'd been.

So why couldn't she let go of it? Physical pleasure was ephemeral, everybody knew that. Love was what stayed with a person—love like she'd felt for Todd.

Darien spent the day trying to recharge her batteries. She would catch up on some correspondence and maybe do some reading, maybe listen to some music.

After breakfast she wrote to her parents. She didn't have anything special to report, but every couple of months she tried to get something in the mail to them. Her mother was pretty good about doing the same. She also jotted a note to Julie Pearson. Again, she had nothing in particular to say, but something called to her to do it. Maybe it was an attempt to reach into her past and make a connection. Nostalgia, perhaps.

Late that afternoon Marc Boudre came to her door with some Italian profiteroles he'd made. "Thought you might like a treat, sweetie," he said. "Something special for dessert."

"Oh, how thoughtful, Marc," she said, taking the cellophane covered plate. "Thank you."

"Seems to me you had them once and enjoyed them, so I thought, why not? They're not ideal for the waistline, but what the heck, a girl needs something to get her mind off her fabulous weekend."

"I *do* need to get my mind off Las Vegas, that's for sure."

"Aren't you going to see him again?"

"I don't think so, Marc."

"Did he say something? I mean, was it clear he just wanted a one-night stand?"

"Come on in," she said, realizing it wasn't a conversation to have standing at the door.

Darien put the pastry in the refrigerator and fixed a pot of tea. She and Marc sat on her love seat to sip their tea and gossip.

"I think you're jumping to conclusions, sweetie," he said when she'd finished, "I truly do. Doesn't sound to me like he had a bad time. By definition, that means he'll be back."

"You really think so?"

"Certainly. Has to be."

"Why did he leave? There wasn't so much as a note. And it's been five days since I've been back. He hasn't tried to contact me."

"That's probably part of the game. He's trying not to be predictable. From the way you describe your weekend, I'd say he considers mystery to be a big part of the fun."

"I think you're being overly optimistic, Marc. It's just as reasonable to conclude he got his rocks off, has had his conquest and has moved on."

Marc considered that. "No, I don't think so. He's planning a surprise. I mean, he had to have read your article. It had to touch him. How could it not?"

Darien put down her cup. "What do you mean by touch him?"

"Sweetie, it was so emotional. I had tears in my eyes. If the man has any heart at all, he did, too. I mean, after all, *he* was there."

"True." Darien thought about what Marc had said. "Lord, I hope he didn't take it as a plea to come back or anything. That wasn't what I was trying to say."

"Not in so many words, but you were nostalgic, wistful. I mean, I just wanted to put my arms around you!"

"Oh, God."

"I know you'll be hearing from him," Marc said, "I know it. He's planning something special. He'll come to the office, swoop you up and carry you off someplace romantic."

"Marc, don't you think there's a chance he doesn't have any romantic impulses at all? Why couldn't he have been in it for the sex, pure and simple?"

"Anything's possible," Marc said, screwing up his face, "but personally I prefer to think that good wishes bring good results. I mean, I'm already thinking in terms of a couple of surrogate grandchildren," he said with a laugh.

After Marc left, Darien settled down with a book, but she couldn't concentrate. She kept wondering if Marc could be right, if Sam was planning a big surprise. She didn't want to think so, because she was afraid to hope. God knows, the last thing she wanted was to risk being disappointed. No, it was easier believing he was gone for good.

Dinnertime came, but she wasn't hungry. She saw no point in consuming calories unnecessarily, so she didn't fix a meal. Around nine she felt a tinge of hunger and got one of Marc's profiteroles from the refrigerator. Sitting at the table alone, eating the pastry, made her think of Sam. She fondly recalled their dinner at Perry's and feeding each other the apple brown Betty. It made her wish he was there with her now.

By ten Darien decided to go to bed, though she rarely hit the sack much before midnight. Happily she fell asleep without much trouble and was dozing restlessly when she half awoke at the sound of a light tapping. It was a minute before she came fully awake. The tapping continued intermittently.

Climbing from her bed, Darien silently made her way to the front room. Who could be knocking at her door in the middle of the night? It couldn't be a burglar, that was for sure. They rarely knocked.

She was able to make out a shadowed figure in the moonlight. A man. Her heart began pounding. There was more knocking. She crept toward the door in the darkness. Through the glass panel next to it she was able to make out the contours of Sam's face.

She unbolted the door and removed the safety latch. She pulled the door open slowly. "Sam?" she whispered. "What are you doing here?"

He put his finger to his lips and slipped inside, closing the door behind him. He was dressed in black like some sort of cat burglar. Darien gazed into his eyes, waiting for him to explain, but he said nothing. But he did run his fingertips over her cheek, making her tremble slightly.

"Sam?" she said tentatively.

Again he put his finger to his lips, indicating she should be quiet. Darien was still half asleep. She knew this wasn't a dream, but she didn't understand it.

Sam pushed her tangled hair off her face and drew his hand down her neck and over her shoulder. He pushed the spaghetti strap of her nightgown off one shoulder, then off the other. The gown slid to the floor, leaving her naked.

The moonlight coming into the cottage was faint, but that didn't stop him from admiring her. He touched her breast, brushing her nipple with feathery strokes of his thumb. Her body responded instantly. She was soon tingling all over, her breathing becoming labored.

He aroused her so quickly that it seemed her body had been predisposed. Perhaps she'd been having an erotic dream.

Darien closed her eyes as Sam caressed her. He moved around her very slowly and she stood motionless, like a statue. When he was behind her, he ran his palm over her buttocks, savoring the curve and the velvety smoothness of her skin.

He still hadn't spoken. All he'd done was touch her. She realized it must be another game, one she didn't understand. But it was clearly calculated to give her pleasure, and it succeeded beautifully.

When she began trembling from a combination of excitement and the coolness of the air, Sam lifted her into his arms and carried her to the bedroom. Then, without a word, he began to undress.

Darien realized he planned to make love with her. She wondered if he'd speak before it was over, or if he intended simply to take his pleasure before dressing and disappearing as quietly as he'd appeared.

When he was naked, he lay beside her. He kissed her first, then ran his hand down over her belly to her mound, finding her moist and ready. He caressed her with his finger until she began to moan. Then he positioned himself between her legs, lifted her knees up over his shoulders and entered her.

He began thrusting immediately. At first the invasion was so unexpected that she wasn't sure she liked it. But then the pleasure made her forget that they weren't making love . . . they were having sex. She began lifting her pelvis against him, meeting his thrusts.

Her orgasm came swiftly. She cried out. Sam covered her mouth, first with his hand, then his lips. He allowed her legs to slide down his body and drop to the bed. He collapsed on her.

For three or four minutes he lay that way until his breathing returned to normal. She was still throbbing faintly when he lifted himself from her. Utterly spent, her body damp with perspiration, she gazed into his dark eyes. For a long minute he looked at her, then got up and dressed.

Once he had his clothes on, Sam gently caressed her face. Then, just as she had anticipated, he stole silently from the room. The last thing she heard was the front door clicking shut behind him.

11

ON SATURDAY, shortly before three in the afternoon, Darien paced her front room, unsure what to expect. The morning after Sam's bizarre midnight visit she'd found a note that said, "I'll pick you up Saturday afternoon around three. Wear a sweater and jeans. Have a change of clothes and whatever else you need to spend the night. Sam."

That annoyed her. Hadn't it occurred to him that Saturday might not be convenient? Had that been the case, she wouldn't have been able to reach him. It would have served him right if she'd gone away and left a note on her door—"So sorry, Sam. I had other plans. Maybe another time."

But of course, she didn't have other plans. And, heaven help her, she did want to see him. She'd become addicted to his damned games. But addicted or not, she was resentful—as much with his cavalier behavior as that she'd fallen victim to it.

She wondered for the hundredth time if this was something he did all the time and she was just his latest victim. Of course, she was probably the first he'd been able to seduce anonymously, but that was one hell of a claim to fame. And no matter how she tried to rationalize it, she was feeling more insecure all the time.

At three o'clock sharp she heard someone coming up the walk. An instant later Sam was at her door. He looked great and he was smiling—the same smile that had charmed her at Perry's and lured her to take risks in Vegas. Despite her dark mood, her fears and her annoyance, she felt her resentment melt. How would she ever be able to resist him?

He had on a bulky fisherman's sweater, pressed jeans and Topsiders without socks. She had on the very same thing. Sam looked her over, as bemused by the coincidence as she.

"There's something very deep at work here," he said. "Suppose the gods are trying to tell us something?"

"Maybe it's a warning."

He smiled. "You look beautiful, by the way."

Darien stood with her hands on her hips. "I see you haven't lost your voice, after all."

He gave her a long, appraising look. "Did you mind?"

"Coming here that way, unannounced, was a little presumptuous, wasn't it?"

"Oh," he said, "I see. Those were cries of protest I was hearing."

"Bastard."

Sam laughed. "I believe fantasy worlds should be rich, diverse and maybe a little unpredictable."

"Any more surprises?" she asked.

"Possibly."

Darien set her overnight case outside the door and stepped to the table to get her purse. When she returned, Sam had the case in his hand. They started down the path that wound through the garden.

"Don't you two look cute!" It was Marc at the back door of the house. He stepped onto the porch.

They stopped.

"Hi, Marc," Darien said.

"I know it's not your long-lost identical twin," Marc said. "He's taller and doesn't look like he could sing soprano."

Darien and Sam laughed. Marc came down the steps and walked over to them.

"You've got to be Sam," he said. "The *San Francisco Bulletin* said you were scrumptious. How many fellows meeting that description can be roaming around in our garden? I'm Marc Boudre," he said, offering his hand.

"And I'm . . ."

Darien noticed that another name almost slipped out before he caught himself.

"Sam," he said, finishing the sentence.

"Sam the mystery man," Marc said. "Well, I won't keep you two. I know you're off on a glorious adventure. Just wanted to say hi." He pinched Darien's cheek. "Be a good girl, sweetie. But that doesn't preclude having fun!" He laughed at his own wit. "Bye," he said, as they headed off.

Sam didn't say anything until they got to the street out front. "Interesting landlord you've got."

"Marc has a partner, Dean. They're wonderful, and very sweet to me, both of them. Marc liked you a lot, I could tell."

"That's not meant to make me uncomfortable, is it?"

"No more than if my mother found you attractive and had an impulse to flirt. Be glad, Sam, they're very protective of me. After all, somebody's got to look out for me."

They'd gone up the street a couple of doors to where a British racing green vintage MG was parked. "Hope you don't mind some wind and sun," he said. "There's a silk scarf in the glove box in case you don't like having your hair blown."

"Where are we going?"

"Up the coast."

"To do what?"

"I thought we should have a nice quiet time together, someplace pleasant where we could relax, enjoy each other's company, get comfortable." He opened the trunk.

"Is this yours?" she asked.

"No, I leased it for the weekend. It's all part of the anonymity," he said with a wink.

He picked up her suitcase and slid it into the small space. Then he opened the passenger door for her and Darien slipped into the seat. She watched him walk around the vehicle and climb in the driver's side. He looked at her.

"You didn't write another article this week," he said. "I wasn't sure if it was a bad sign or not."

"I'm not sure myself," she said, staring straight ahead.

"Is this something we need to talk about?"

There seemed to be genuine concern in his voice and it surprised her. "Maybe. But it doesn't have to be now. We'll have time, if this is going to be a quiet weekend, like you say."

"Until now all I've had to do was pick up the paper to find out what you were thinking."

"I'm beginning to think I've run out the string on this particular series."

He considered that. "Does that mean you've run out the string on Sam, as well?"

Darien opened the glove compartment and removed the scarf. She noticed it was a Hermès. "I suppose that's something we can talk about," she said, as she tied the scarf around her head.

"Sounds ominous."

"Good honest communication needn't be," she said.

Sam considered that for a moment, then removed a checkered short-billed cap from the door pocket and slipped it on his head. He put on sunglasses, then started the engine. It sputtered for a moment, but soon settled into a nice smooth purr. He gave her a lazy smile, as if to signal that everything was just fine. Darien smiled back.

Sam took her hand and pulled it to his mouth, kissing it. "There's not a woman in the world with whom I'd rather get caught in public wearing matching outfits."

"Do you think we look silly?"

"No. But even if we did, it doesn't matter. There won't be anybody but us where we're going."

The remark could have bothered her, but after his midnight visit, the prospect of being alone with him didn't have much sting. Actually, she was intrigued with what he had in mind. Already the mood was entirely different from the last two times she'd seen him. He was more like the Sam she'd had dinner with at Perry's—a regular kind of guy, albeit a charming and alluring one.

They took off down the street and Darien was seized with the exhilaration of the adventure. Whatever his mood or mask, she'd discovered there was nothing predictable about Sam—unless it was being unpredictable.

It was a wonderful sunny day with a cooling ocean breeze. Darien couldn't recall being in a convertible since college. The boy she'd dated before Todd, a fellow whose name she'd forgotten, had an old Mustang that he liked to drive around in the company of a pretty girl. They'd gone out four or five times, but she remembered the car better than she remembered him.

The Saturday traffic was heavy, though unlike commute days, it bore no particular pattern. They made it to Doyle Drive in good time and were soon on the Golden Gate Bridge. As they were crossing it, Darien looked straight up at the towers, having a better sense of their majesty in an open car. They continued through Marin, and when they came to the Tiburon Boulevard turnoff she glanced toward the town. When she turned back she noticed that Sam had been looking at her.

"I'm going to remember that day for a long time, too," he said.

"How did you know that's what I was thinking about?"

"I don't know. Maybe because you were looking in that direction."

"It started my fourth decade off in an interesting fashion," she said. "I'll say that."

"I'm sorry I was oblivious to you at the time."

Darien studied his profile. It was the angle she'd seen him that day. Visually he was sublime, but the man on the deck at Sam's had been a creature of her imagination. Oddly enough, he was now a person in his own right, but one without a history or a context, except as her companion and cocreator of her fantasies.

"Can I ask you a question?" she said.

"Sure, ask away."

"What were you doing that day at Sam's? Why were you there alone?"

He stared up the highway. "I felt like getting out of the house, so I took off and went where my nose took me."

"Do you live alone?"

He turned and looked at her, his expression surprisingly sober. "Does it matter? I mean, the truth behind the facade is secondary to the facade, if it counts at all. Sam is what counts and Sam is who I am."

She considered that, watching the traffic ahead. "I wish I didn't feel that you were being evasive."

"Do you want to talk about me, Darien? Is that what you're suggesting?"

She came very close to saying, "Yes, I want to know who you are. I want the details of your life from the very first memory you had as a child. I want to know all about you. The hell with Sam, the hell with this game, the hell with the *Bulletin*."

"Well?" he said, when she said nothing.

Darien shook her head. "No, it would just get in the way. As they say, if it ain't broke, don't fix it."

"It's your call," he said. "Anytime you want to know, all you have to do is ask."

"Really? I mean, are you really willing to come out of the closet, so to speak?"

"I am unless it would ruin our relationship."

She said nothing to that because she didn't know what to say. Dealing with Sam, an anonymous lover, was one thing, but to give herself to a real live somebody, with a history and a life, somebody with needs and expectations beyond sex, was something else altogether. Anyway, he might not be sincere. He could have said that for effect.

"Is that a meaningful silence?" he asked over the rush of the wind.

"Let me give it some thought."

"Somehow, I figured that's what you'd say."

He didn't seem upset. She scooted down and leaned her head back, staring at the pale blue sky. She wondered if he might not be relieved. After all, what more could a guy wish for than what she'd willingly given? For that matter, what more could she ask of him?

They drove up U.S. 101 to Cotati and then followed State Route 116 to Sebastopol. From there they took the Bodega Highway to the coast, passing through a valley surrounded by rolling oak-studded hills. It had been quite warm inland, but when they came onto the coastal plain, the air became much cooler. At the town of Bodega Bay the sun grew faint in a haze that became a filmy fog in places.

The coast highway was jammed with day-trippers, which detracted some from the ambience. But once they were past Jenner-by-the-Sea, the traffic thinned.

Darien had never been up the coast before, though Maryanne often spoke of the scenery, which she described as both lovely and dramatic. When the twisting highway began climbing a sheer sea cliff, Darien saw what Maryanne meant. They were a thousand feet above the ocean. The view extended fifty miles. But Darien was not fond of heights. About the only thing to be grateful for was that they were on the cliff side of the highway.

"Quite a view, isn't it?" Sam said.

"Yes, but I hate the thought of driving home. There aren't even guard rails on a lot of these curves."

He chuckled. "I suppose we can drive back in the dark. That way you won't be able to see how far down it is."

"Thanks loads. The edge of the road will be on my side of the car."

"Yes, but wherever your half of the car goes, mine is sure to follow."

"Great. You're saying if we die, we die together."

Sam nodded. "Yeah, something like that."

"Very reassuring." Darien gripped the door handle as the MG twisted around a particularly sharp curve. "Sam, I don't mean to disillusion you, but this cliff fits into my nightmares better than my fantasies."

"You should have told me you're afraid of heights."

"You know now," she said, gritting her teeth as a truck appeared suddenly from around a blind curve ahead.

"They say there's nothing like an adrenaline rush to heighten your sex drive," he said, glancing over.

"As I recall, yours was adequate in low gear. Just keep your eye on the road, please."

He chuckled, gearing down for the next curve.

Mercifully the sea cliff soon dropped down to a level plain. The road straightened out and there was terra firma on both sides of the highway. Darien was able to breathe for the first time in half an hour.

Before long they came to Sea Ranch. It was a community of modern homes spread over thousands of acres of coastline, spaced out for privacy and to take advantage of the views. It might have been an exclusive suburb except for the fact that it was a hundred miles from San Francisco. Beyond Sea Ranch was the town of Gualala. Once little more than a few scattered buildings, it now claimed a small shopping center with stores and restaurants. Sam told her it was the only civilization of consequence between Point Arena and Bodega Bay, a stretch of nearly seventy miles.

The landscape had been barren, rocky, bleak and windswept south of Sea Ranch, but it was more forested and green as they traveled north. Above Gualala the pine woods ran down from the coastal hills to the water's edge. The sun was brighter and it seemed warmer to Darien, as well.

"How much farther?" she asked.

"Just a few miles. Need to stop?"

"I'm good for a few more miles. Are we going to be camping out, or what?"

"It's a little weekend place . . . with indoor plumbing, you'll be glad to know."

"Do you come here often?"

"No."

She'd come to expect uninformative answers, so she didn't press. At least this time he was talking. That taciturn visit he'd made to her cottage had been perversely arousing, and more than a little kinky, but she hardly wanted a steady diet of it. On the other hand the outgoing, loquacious Sam could be just as confounding and unpredictable.

Before long he slowed the car, turning into a drive on the ocean side of the highway that was guarded by a high iron gate. There was a stone wall that hid the property from view, not that much could be seen for the thick forest. Sam punched a code into the electric control panel and the gate swung open.

"Does this mean I can expect both hot and cold running water?" Darien said ironically.

Sam grinned. "You aren't an elitist, Ms. Hughes, are you?"

"No, I have simple needs. Flush toilets are appreciated, though."

He put the car in gear and they drove down a twisting drive into the woods. Soon Darien saw broken glimpses of the ocean through the trees. Then the house came into view. It was starkly modern with irregular angles of wood and glass, and it was huge. It was built on a rocky promontory a hundred feet above the Pacific. Trees grew right up to the front door, but there had to be a hundred and eighty degrees of ocean view in the back.

"Some cabin," Darien said as they came to a stop out front.

"Weekend homes are meant to be different."

They got out and Darien stretched, all the while admiring the architectural wonder before her. Sam opened the trunk, a mischievous smile on his face.

"Be honest. Is this place yours?"

"Is that your first question for the day?"

"You still owe me one from Las Vegas. I never asked my third. So just answer the question, damn it. I want to know."

"All right, the answer is no."

"Too bad," she said, looking at the angular lines of the structure.

"Ironically, I had a chance to buy this place a few months ago, but I decided it was too far from the city. Do you think I made a mistake?"

Though he didn't say it, she wondered if he was really asking if it was the sort of place she could imagine herself sharing with him. God knows, that was the question she asked herself. It was the first time she'd thought about them being together as a couple, and it unnerved her a little that she'd taken that step. "I don't know," she said, still looking at the intricate wood and stonework on the facade.

"It was that slow drive more than the actual distance," he said.

Then Darien remembered the cliff that seemed to drop off to eternity. "Maybe if you had a helicopter . . ."

"I should have considered that. Well, have a look at the inside and see what you think." He took a basket from the trunk and handed it to her. "Would you mind carrying the provisions?"

He took her suitcase and his overnight bag, then led the way up the steps, which turned at a landing. Ferns grew on either side of the redwood stairs. The front door was extremely tall and very heavy. Sam unlocked it.

The inside of the house was even more dramatic than the outside. The ceiling was open and soared two stories. From the entry there were four steps down to the main living area with an enormous stone fireplace at one end. The back of the house was almost entirely glass and looked out over the sea. At either end of the wide steps were beds of ferns. Between the stone, the wood, the vegetation and the view of the ocean, the architect had brought the outdoors inside. Back from the entry a staircase wound up to the upper floor where the bedrooms were located, but Darien was drawn down the stairs, to the great room. Sam left the cases in the entry and followed her.

The furniture was modern, clean and geometric in design. It looked comfortable and inviting. The room was accented with more large plants and huge geometric oils in bold colors.

"Wow," Darien said as she gazed around, "this might even be worth the drive along that cliff."

"You *must* be impressed."

She gave him a look. "Does it live up to the standard of your fantasies?" he asked.

"Honey, in *my* fantasies this place belongs to *me*, not you."

"You wouldn't share?"

"If you provided the helicopter."

"We may have the makings of a deal here."

"Dream on," she said.

"Well, it's ours for the weekend."

"I think you'd best point me toward the plumbing."

"There's a powder room in the entry and two more bathrooms upstairs."

"I might as well take my suitcase up."

"I'll take it for you," he said.

"No, even in my fantasies I don't need to be waited on hand and foot. But thanks."

"I'll put the champagne on ice and get the perishables in the fridge."

"Sam," she said, before turning away.

"Yes?"

"Have you ever brought another woman here?"

"I'll have to charge you for that one," he said.

"That's all right. I want to know."

"Does it make a difference if I have?"

"I guess it doesn't," she said, "but I want to know anyway."

He shrugged. "You're the first."

"The trailblazer, in other words."

"Do I seem like a beginner, somebody formulating a technique?" he asked.

"Maybe we should leave this one," she said. "I don't really care about your past. Or your future, either. Fantasies don't work that way."

"There's only the here and now, is that it?"

"Something like that."

"You're the boss. I'm but your humble servant, the instrument of your will."

"You're also full of it," she said with a grin. "But forgivable. Now if you'll excuse me. Nature calls."

Darien went upstairs. There was an enormous master suite and two small guest rooms. She stuck her head into one of the guest rooms. Judging by the decor it was sometimes occupied by a small boy. The master suite was sumptuous and offered a view of the Pacific. There was little evidence that it was occupied on a regular basis. It wasn't quite as impersonal as a hotel room, but neither was it anyone's unqualified domain.

There were a couple of clothes bags in the closet, a drawer of toiletries in the bath and two framed photos on a dresser, one of a boy of six or seven, the other of a blond woman in her mid-thirties. The woman was chic without being pretty. It all meant something to someone, but Darien had no idea what.

After she'd refreshed herself, she made her way downstairs. Sam was on a glass-enclosed deck, staring at the spectacular view. The sun was low on the horizon, the colors of sunset beginning to gather. He'd put a bottle of champagne in an ice bucket to chill. Hearing her, he turned.

"Ah, the last piece of the puzzle. Scenes like this can't be fully appreciated alone."

Darien moved next to him and he put his arm around her. He kissed her hair. She sighed. "It's beautiful, absolutely beautiful."

"I'd planned a picnic for dinner. Thought maybe we could eat out here. It's almost like being outside, minus the wind and cool air. Champagne is on ice, as you can see."

"Champagne has become our signature, hasn't it?"

"If you'd prefer something else, I can run into Gualala. It would only take me fifteen minutes."

"No, no, champagne's fine. I was just remarking."

"The results have been pretty good so far."

Darien stared at a freighter on the distant horizon. "I hope you don't regard this as a performance," she said. "I know given the game we're playing a certain amount of staging is necessary, but I hate to think what you do is forced...."

Sam took her by the shoulders and turned her toward him. "Did I say the wrong thing? Are you upset with me?"

She shook her head. "No, I sometimes get confused between what's supposed to be real and what's supposed to be fiction. I said that impulsively."

"Well, what exactly did you mean?"

"I didn't mean anything."

He lifted her chin. "Yes, you did."

Darien sighed.

"Maybe I'm trying too hard," he said.

"It's nothing, Sam, really. I just have to keep reminding myself that you're an actor and that I'm an actress."

"I'm not getting paid to do this, you know," he said.

"Then why are you doing it?"

"Because I like being with you. Last weekend was one of the most enjoyable of my life. And this one promises to be as well."

"Let's be frank, you liked the sex."

"Yes, I did. I won't apologize for liking it, either. But that's not all, by a long shot."

She smiled. "Keep that up and your nose will grow."

"I can prove it."

"Oh, yeah? How?"

"We'll make this a celibate weekend. Lots of romance and affection. No sex."

"That's more of a threat than a promise."

He laughed. "You aren't making this easy for me."

"Maybe we should erase the tape and start over," Darien said.

Sam looked back at her intently, trying hard to understand what she wanted from him.

"In case you haven't figured it out yet," she said, "women are supposed to be this way. If we fit perfectly into your system of logic, there would be no mystery."

"You know, that's the clearest explanation of the problem I've heard yet," he said. Then he kissed her on the lips.

It started out tender, but quickly grew passionate. When she finally broke it off her heart was pounding and her body was asking for more. "Thank goodness we didn't decide on celibacy. I don't have that kind of will-power." Patting his cheek, she slipped from his arms and went to the end of the enclosed sun room. Outside on the open deck was a spa. "Does that thing work?" she asked.

"Sure. Just takes a little time to heat it up. Shall I turn it on?"

She shrugged. "Frankly, I've never been in one. They aren't as common in New York as they are in California."

"And they aren't common in Bos . . ." His voice trailed off.

Darien spun around, her eyes wide. "You're from Boston!"

"I didn't say that."

"You almost did. That's what you were going to say. Come on, Sam, admit it! I'm from Amherst originally, you know! When did you leave Boston?"

He gave her a look.

"Ha! I knew you'd slip up eventually!" She chortled gleefully.

He looked crestfallen. Darien took compassion on him and went over and took his hand.

"It's all right if you're somebody, a *real* somebody, I mean."

"I thought you liked the anonymity."

"I do," she said, "but a glimpse at whoever it is behind this act is . . ."

"Is what?"

"I don't know . . . reassuring, maybe."

"You mean you don't mind if I'm a real person, after all?"

"No, I don't mind," she said, but she knew her tone wasn't terribly convincing.

He kissed her on the temple and stepped past her to open the door to the deck. "I'll turn on the spa for later."

Darien watched him. When he returned she said, "Who are the woman and the boy upstairs?"

"Woman and boy?"

"In the pictures."

"Oh."

"Well?"

He gave her a wry look. "That isn't a yes or no question."

"Are they yours?"

"That'll be your second," he warned.

"My first today. The last one was left over from Vegas."

"They aren't mine. They're friends."

"From Boston, too?" she asked.

"No, they aren't, but you'd better stop asking questions or you'll use up a month's worth before dinner."

"You can't count the one about Boston."

"All right. But no more freebies."

"I do have one I want you to answer," she said.

"You're sure? It'll just leave you one."

She nodded. "Do you have a terrible dark secret this game is enabling you to keep from me?"

"What kind of secret?"

"I don't know, something that would put my teeth on edge. Like you're really a Mafia don, or you have wives in three states."

"Nothing like that, no."

"No dark secrets at all?" she persisted.

"Everybody has their secrets, Darien. You have yours, I'm sure. But if it's reassurance you're seeking, you needn't worry."

"Can I trust you?"

"Yes. Now you've used up your questions for the day, my dear. I'm sorry. You'll have to wait until tomorrow."

"Oh, great," she chided, "tomorrow, if I ask if you're a compulsive liar, you'll admit it and then I'll know everything you've said today was a lie."

"Then I'd better do a pretty good job tonight, hadn't I?"

Darien put her hands on her hips. "You are the smoothest son of a gun I've ever met, Mr...." Her shoulders slumped. "See, I don't even know what to call you. Give me a last name. You can do that much!"

"Smith."

"Bastard."

"No, I like Smith better," he said.

She took a swing at him. Sam ducked, then grabbed her from behind, giving her a big bear hug. He kissed her neck, drawing his tongue up behind her ear, making her shiver.

"Getting hungry?" he whispered in her ear.

"For what?"

"I was thinking of dinner, but I'll let you answer the question any way you want."

"I think I'd like to go out to the point for a close-up view of the ocean."

"Nothing like salt air to enhance the appetite," he agreed.

"You are incorrigible, Mr. Smith."

"I know," he said, "it's all part of the master plan."

"What master plan?"

He tapped the tip of her nose with his finger. "I'm afraid you'll just have to wait and see, my love. You'll just have to wait and see."

12

"I WON'T feel like I've been to the ocean unless I wade in the water and feel the sand in my toes," she said as they'd stood on the point watching the sun drop toward the horizon.

"Be my guest," he replied, "but this kid doesn't get near the water unless we're talking the Caribbean or Tahiti, or some other place where it's warm enough to take a bath."

"Chicken."

"My lifeguard skills are rusty, so be careful," he said.

Darien gave him a look and started making her way down the path that led to the tiny cove. At each turn she glanced at him. Once he waved and she waved back.

The mood of this fantasy adventure was certainly different, and she wasn't sure what to attribute it to. Was this the real Sam? Was his true nature playful and gentle, or was he the bon vivant, man-about-town she'd been with in Las Vegas? The dark, mysterious lover or the regular, fun-loving guy? Or was it that none of those personas was real? Maybe she hadn't yet seen the man he truly was. Maybe she never would.

Coming out from behind a large rock, she heard him call to her. "Careful of the surf," he said, "that lake out there is Pacific in name only."

"I practically grew up on Cape Cod," she called back. "I know all about waves."

He shrugged and she continued on, soon coming to the edge of the sandy beach. Sitting down, she took off her shoes and rolled up her pant legs. She looked at the point and saw him standing where she'd left him.

For some reason that image of him brought to mind another day, years earlier, when she'd gone with Todd to Maine to meet his family. He and his father had gone out sailing, despite unusually heavy seas. She'd decided to stay behind, but she'd gone to the dock to see them off. When they returned safely, Todd was rosy-cheeked and windblown, but none the worse for wear. Yet when she reflected on his death, she often thought of the time she'd watched him sail away, knowing it had been like that on the day he died.

Her love for Todd would always have a poignant cast because of the tragedy that ended his life. Lately, though, she'd tried analyzing their relationship critically. They'd been young and in love, of course, but what she felt at the time seemed almost . . . immature. True, she'd given Todd everything she had to give, but she was a different woman now, capable of giving more. And she demanded more from a relationship now, too. A lot more.

Still, she couldn't help wondering what life would be like if Todd had lived. They'd have grown—she hoped together—but she didn't think their relationship would have the edge, the excitement, she'd found with Sam.

Sam was one of a kind. And were it not for a most bizarre turn of events, they never would have gotten together. What she wasn't sure of was if this sexual being she'd turned into would have lain dormant forever if they hadn't met. It was difficult to believe one man could make such a difference. More likely it was a combination of things, the fantasy foremost among them.

She strolled around the cove, letting the gentle waves lap her ankles. The water was icy, but she liked the feel of wet sand between her toes and the sting of the tangy salt air on her face.

"You must have ice in your veins," Sam called to her.

"Is that an allusion to my personality?"

"I was referring to the water."

"It is pretty cold."

He put his hand to his ear, signaling he hadn't heard.

"I said, it *is* pretty cold."

"There's a current out there that comes all the way down from Alaska. If you want to play in that stuff, you should have a wet suit."

"You don't have one in a size eight by any chance, do you?"

"No. If you want to swim, you'll have to skinny dip. Nobody can see into the cove unless it's a passing freighter and they'd be too far away to see much."

"What about you?"

"I'll close my eyes."

Darien waved him off and turned toward the breakers rolling in. Whether it was because she hadn't been paying enough attention to where she was walking, or because she'd gotten complacent, she wasn't sure, but she was farther into the water than she should have been, and an unusually large wave was bearing down on her.

Sam shouted to her to watch out. She spun to run to higher ground but caught her toe on a half-buried rock. Falling flat on her face in the wet sand, she was covered almost instantly by the wave. As it receded she climbed to her feet, sputtering.

She was dripping from head to toe and beginning to shiver when Sam got to her side. He was breathless from having hurried.

"Don't say a word," she warned, shaking her finger at him. "I feel enough like a jerk without you saying I told you so."

"They say lessons are learned best when they're learned through experience."

"Oh, shut up!"

He chuckled, but not too hard. She was sure she'd turned blue. She had to get out of her wet clothes.

"Want me to help you on with your shoes?" he asked.

"No, I'd rather you carry me up to the house."

"Sorry," he said, shaking his head, "I don't do those kind of fantasies. I'm strictly into pleasure."

She smiled through her misery, her teeth chattering. "Don't you know slaying dragons is as important as wine and roses?"

"A hot tub is my best offer, but you've got to walk."

Darien dropped to the ground to put on her shoes. "Women's lib certainly has its limitations," she grumbled.

Once she had her shoes on, he helped her up and brushed sand from her cheek. Then he took her hand. "Come on, Shamu," he said, and began pulling her up the path.

"I hope the water in that hot tub is hot," she said as she squished along.

"I'll volunteer my services as a lifeguard," he said.

"Damned decent of you, Sam. Where were you when I really needed you?"

"I told you, I'm into hot water."

"In more ways than one, Mr. Smith. In more ways than one." She slung water from her dripping sleeve at him. "You're lucky I don't have a garden hose."

"Do you always get this testy after a swim in the ocean?" he asked.

Darien took a swing at him, but he hooted and skipped away. She started chasing him and they ended up running all the way to the house.

BY THE TIME she climbed onto the deck, her chest heaving from the exertion of the run, Sam had already gotten a couple of big fluffy beach towels from the cabinet at the far end of the deck.

"Let me help you off with that sweater," he said, his voice more serious now.

"That really... took it... out of me," she gasped.

"It was probably good to keep your blood circulating," he said, lifting the sweater over her head. "Soaked, this thing weighs a ton."

"Tell me about it."

Sam went to the edge of the deck and wrung her sweater out over the rail while Darien kicked off her shoes and unfastened her jeans. He returned and helped balance her while she peeled off her jeans. She was still breathing hard, but shivering at the same time.

"God, I've never been so cold," she said, glancing at the steamy water in the bubbling spa. "I hope that's as warm as it looks."

"It's going to feel scalding when you get in, so be prepared."

Darien unfastened her bra without giving modesty a second thought. Her panties followed. Right then she would have jumped in a pool full of alligators, if the water was hot. She went to the edge of the tub. Sam helped her sit down. She put her feet in first then, after a second's pause, slipped in, standing waist deep.

"You're right, it's hot as hell," she said. But, like a lobster eager to be eaten, she sank down to her chin. The water felt as if it might burn her at first, but then her body adjusted and it started feeling wonderful. "Ah, heaven," she said.

"You look a little more contented than you did a few moments ago."

"Sam, I forgive you all your sins for having the foresight to heat this thing."

"Does that mean I can join you?"

"I'm willing to give you my soul as well as my body." She purred. "This is better than sex."

"Well, let's not overdramatize," he said, removing his sweater.

Darien watched him undress, admiring his physique in the fading light of dusk. When he was stripped naked he climbed into the tub, sliding around the perimeter until his hip and shoulder bumped up against hers.

He lightly kissed her on the lips. "Hell of a way to get a woman out of her clothes."

"Another technique to add to your repertoire," she said.

"Does my repertoire need expanding?"

She patted his knee. "I don't think so. So far, big boy, you seem to be doing just fine."

"I'm pleased milady thinks so. But one rose does not a summer make."

"Meaning?" she asked.

"That you ain't seen nothin' yet."

Darien smiled secretly. "You mean *now*, while I'm still weak with cold and unable to properly defend myself?"

He leaned over to give her another kiss. "I'll let you warm up first. In fact, feel free to get as hot as you want."

The way he said it made her think about Las Vegas—especially the way he had waited for her to ask to be taken. Then later, when he was making love to her, how he'd kept her on the edge, waiting until she was ready to come before satisfying himself.

Darien took a deep breath. She might not know a whole hell of a lot about his background—except that he was probably from Boston and had more money than he knew what to do with—but she was learning more about him as a man all the time. He was an exciting and accomplished lover who knew how to be considerate as well as enigmatic. But his appeal went beyond that. With each hour they were together, that became more and more apparent. She liked Sam for more than his body and his ability to satisfy her. Maybe it was just her natural feminine proclivity to look beyond the physical, but she was beginning to care. A whole lot.

As she was thinking about her feelings, Sam put his arm around her shoulders and gathered her close. She scooted farther down in the tub and leaned her head against his arm, liking the feel of him next to her. It was amazing how comfortable she was starting to feel with him. But then it occurred to her she shouldn't get too comfortable with the way he was. Tomorrow he could be a different man entirely.

The water didn't feel nearly so hot now and she was no longer shivering. Darien absently rubbed her leg against Sam's. They stayed that way for quite a while, neither saying anything, just relaxing in the soothing bubbles of the spa.

After a while he began caressing her, rubbing his hands over her legs and breasts. He kissed her neck and ear and eyes. And when she responded by eagerly kissing him, he pulled her onto his lap so that she straddled him. As they kissed, he slipped his finger inside her. She immediately took his penis in her hand.

"I'm not going to keep this up for long if you keep doing that," he said, poking his tongue into his cheek.

She gave him a little jab with her elbow, then she kissed his mouth. "What do you suggest we do instead?"

In answer to her question he put his hands on her waist and lifted her over his erection. Then he slowly lowered her until he was deep inside her. For a moment they stayed like that, savoring the feel of being connected. But neither of them was able to keep from moving for long.

She put her hands on Sam's shoulders and he gripped her hips. He was long and hard as he slid in and out of her. Darien leaned her head back and shut her eyes. Her world was reduced to the sound of the bubbles churning in the spa and the feel of Sam inside her. Everything else seemed to fade away. There were no other sounds, no other sensations.

Within moments they were both ready to come. Darien called out his name, begging him to do it now. He thrust a final time, nearly lifting her from the water.

Afterward neither of them said anything for a long, long time. They just floated together, completely spent. Finally Sam spoke.

"I don't know about you, but if we don't get out of this thing soon we'll turn into prunes."

"I know," she said. "It's just that I'm not sure I'll ever be able to move again."

He kissed her cheek and gently lifted her off him. She felt the water swish between her legs and she suddenly felt bereft—as if she was incomplete now that Sam was no longer a part of her.

Sam climbed out of the spa. He went over to grab a couple of towels. After wrapping one around his waist, he held out the other for Darien as she stepped onto the deck. She was still so warm after being in the water that the air didn't even seem cool.

Sam turned off the spa and the sound of the machinery died. Darien could hear the waves crashing against the rocks out on the point.

As they went inside the house, she said, "My hair is full of sand. I'll need to take a shower."

"I wouldn't mind taking one myself. I don't like all the chemicals they have to put in the spa."

He took her hand as they headed upstairs. The master bathroom was huge. Darien went to her suitcase and grabbed her robe, the hair dryer and the shampoo. By the time she got to the bathroom Sam was already in the shower. She knocked on the clear glass as he shampooed his hair.

"Is there room for one more in there?" she asked.

He opened the door. "You bet. You can do my back."

"Really? And what will you do?" she asked.

He grinned. "Anything milady wants."

She dropped her towel and stepped in. The water was hot, though not as hot as in the spa. She opened the shampoo bottle and put a big glob on her head. Before she could start working it through her hair, Sam took over.

Darien stepped directly in front of the shower and he stood behind her, washing her hair. After he rinsed the shampoo out he grabbed the soap, handed it over and turned away from her.

She carefully lathered her hands before her fingers began caressing the back of his neck. Sam groaned with pleasure. "You know," he said, "I think I could get used to this."

"You mean you don't keep someone at home to scrub your back when you've put in a hard day...uh, well, doing whatever it is you do?"

"Haven't you already run out of questions?"

"You can put it on my account."

"I don't keep anyone around to rub my back." He rolled his head to get out a couple of kinks. "But I might start taking job applications. Interested?"

Darien chuckled. "I don't think so." She began massaging the soap into his lower back. When she skimmed the top of his buttocks, he groaned again.

"I'll offer double what the *Bulletin*'s paying you."

"Yes, but there's no future in it. I think I'll stick to the writing game," she said, trailing her finger along the crease in his buttocks, "and you can stick to night games, since that seems to be where your talents lie."

With that, Sam turned abruptly and took her into his arms. As Darien backed up against the tile she kissed him, hard. He opened his mouth and she traced the edge of his teeth with her tongue. At almost the same time, Sam put his hand between them and drew his middle finger across her opening. But this time, instead of teasing her, he immediately slipped his finger inside and began to pleasure her.

Darien moaned. She spread her legs farther apart and kept on kissing him. When he pulled away from her mouth to suck her breasts, she knew she couldn't hold back any longer. She came like that, leaning against the wall, the spray hitting her full in the face as Sam sucked her nipples.

She'd have stayed that way forever if her legs could have supported her, but it was all she could do to stand. Sam helped her out of the shower stall, then dried her with a fluffy, soft towel. Darien slipped on her robe as he toweled himself off.

"Getting hungry?" he asked.

"For what?"

Sam smiled. "I was thinking food, but this is your fantasy, my love."

Darien rolled her eyes. "You may have to carry me to the table." She ran a comb through her wet hair, too exhausted to deal with the hair dryer. "Unless you'd be offended, I'm not going to fool with my hair until morning."

"I'm not that easily offended. Besides, we've got a lot more fantasy to live out. Let's make the most of it."

DARIEN AWOKE around two in the morning. Sam was sleeping peacefully beside her, his breathing slow and even. For a time she listened to it, then she became aware of the sound of the waves crashing into the rocks on the point. The soothing rhythm of the sea and the cool air were coming in the open window across the room.

Once again Sam had been the perfect lover, satisfying her in a way she hadn't thought possible. She couldn't have conjured up anyone better. And yet she felt uneasy, wary, afraid.

She'd come to realize that Sam was a mixed blessing. His virtues were the problem. Sex was too good with him. He made her want more, always more. He could ruin lovemaking with anyone else if she wasn't careful.

The notion was ironic, considering. Her initial intent had been to put excitement in her life, have an adventure while she gathered material for her articles and . . . well, yes, to have some pleasure along the way.

But in every way imaginable, Sam had proven to be more than what she'd bargained for. His night games were turning her into a sensualist. In short, he had created a monster.

The question now was how long could she allow this to go on? Not long, that was certain. Yet, even as she told herself that, she thought of the joy he'd brought her. It wasn't just physical pleasure, either. The best fantasies went beyond that—and Sam certainly did. He'd outdone himself. At the time, she was sure that nothing could top what he'd done to her in the spa or the shower. But she'd underestimated his imagination.

They'd had dinner lying by the fire, drinking wine and eating brie, caviar, smoked salmon, grapes and berries. As they'd eaten, they'd watched the flickering flames. Even before they'd finished, he'd made love to her again. The memory would be with her forever. They had just finished the champagne when Sam parted her robe and smeared a big gob of caviar across her breasts. Then, as she watched, he slowly and carefully licked every bit of it off.

It was the idea of what he was doing, even more than the actual sensation, that really turned her on. When she'd begged him to take her, he'd taken the belt out of her robe and lightly tied her hands together. Then, after pulling her hands over her head, he tied the other end of the belt to the foot of a wing chair.

Darien had never been tied up before. And even though she could have gotten free if she'd wanted to badly enough, the idea of it was incredibly sexy. She'd felt helpless, totally at the mercy of her senses and Sam's imagination. He had not let her down. She'd writhed under him, her hands straining against her bonds, amazed by the excitement of the sensation. By the time they'd come and he'd finally untied her, she was sure that no matter how long she lived, nothing, absolutely nothing, could ever top that.

When they'd come up to bed they had made love the final time. He'd been gentle and loving then. He'd told her he loved her with his body, if not his words, and the impossibility of it all made her want to cry. Tears had filled her eyes because she knew it was too wonderful to go on. If she let it continue, it would end badly. That much was certain.

It was up to her to bring things to a graceful close. The fantasy was hers and ultimate control lay in her hands.

Having resolved to take action, she felt a tremendous sense of relief. She'd sleep now that the decision was made. That's what her subconscious had been waiting for—completion.

Darien didn't awake until she felt someone sit on the bed. As she opened her eyes to the bright morning sun, the aroma of coffee hit her. She lifted her head.

"How about some breakfast in bed?"

Sam was cleaned up and dressed. Darien rubbed her eyes. "What time is it?"

"A little after nine."

"I slept in."

"I noticed. I showered, drove into town for a newspaper and some orange juice, took a walk in the woods and decided you'd slept enough."

"I have. Sorry to be such a sleepyhead."

She'd slept naked. Now that it was morning and their night games were over, she felt shy about sitting up and having coffee bare-breasted.

"Maybe I'll run to the bathroom first," she said. Slipping from under the covers, she scampered toward the bath, pausing to snatch her robe from the top of her suitcase. When she returned, she had it on. "Have you eaten?" she asked, getting into bed.

"Yes, but I thought I'd have some coffee with you."

She fluffed some pillows and pulled the covers up over her legs. Sam set the tray on her lap. Then he kissed her on the temple.

"I take it you slept well."

"I was awake for a while during the night."

"I hope it wasn't my snoring."

"No," she said, shaking her head.

She examined the tray. There was a glass of orange juice, a plate of croissants, a bowl of strawberries and coffee.

"This is very thoughtful of you, Sam."

"Life is the small things as well as the large," he said.

Darien took a long drink, then put down the glass. "Funny to think how little I know about your philosophy and values," she said. "A certain amount is evident from the way you behave, but it's hard to know someone when they're just a fantasy character."

"I stand ready to become the real me. All you have to do is say the word."

She wondered if he sounded forthright because he wanted to seem confident, or if it was because he wanted to keep the burden on her. "Aren't you a little scared what might happen?"

"No, not at all. Are you?"

She hesitated. "Maybe. I don't think I'm ready."

There was consternation on his face, but if he wanted to say anything he restrained himself. One thing she had to hand him—Sam always kept his word. She tried to focus on the resolve she'd mustered in the middle of the night and found she was less sure of herself by light of day. She gave herself a silent pep talk, knowing she had to stick to her guns.

"I'll trust you to tell me when you are ready," he said.

Darien took a big bite of croissant, nodding. Sam watched her eat in silence for a while. "I've been giving some thought to next weekend," he said. "I've got one or two ideas up my sleeve."

"We don't have to decide anything now."

His eyes narrowed and he looked at her for a long time before he responded. "What are you saying? That you'd rather not talk about it?"

"No, just that we don't have to decide right now. I don't want you to feel like you have to come up with some sensational adventure."

He seemed mollified by her remark. She sipped some coffee. Sam got up and went to the window to look out at the ocean.

"I should get back to the city at a decent hour," he said. "I've got a meeting in the morning that I'll have to prepare for this evening, and it's a long drive."

She wondered what sort of meeting, what he did for a living. It would have been natural to ask, but it was not the direction she wanted things to go. "I understand," she said. "Getting back early's good for me, too."

"I guess you have an article to write, don't you?" he said.

"Yes, I do."

Sam was peering out at the view again. He turned from the window. "There's no big rush," he said. "Get ready at your own pace. We can stop somewhere along the way for lunch. Maybe in Tiburon, at Sam's." He smiled.

"Stopping for lunch is not necessary," she said. "If I have breakfast, I usually don't eat again until dinner, so don't do it for me."

Sam stuck his hands in his pockets. "Well, we can play it by ear." He gestured toward her tray. "Want more coffee?"

"No, thanks. I'm fine."

He contemplated her, looking as though he had something he wanted to say. "Well," he said after several moments, "I'll go downstairs. I've got a couple of phone calls to make. We can leave when you're ready."

"Half an hour or so is all I need."

Sam nodded, smiling blandly. "Fine." He left the room.

Darien picked up her cup, but put it down without taking a sip. She'd suddenly lost her appetite. Setting the tray aside, she gazed out at the gray-blue sky. She knew then that she couldn't drag this out too much longer. She would have to end it. And soon.

13

THE DRIVE BACK to the Bay Area felt as if it was taking forever. If Sam sensed the tension in her, he didn't mention it. They didn't talk a great deal.

It had been foggy as they'd driven along the treacherous stretch of road high on the sea cliff, and she hadn't been able to see the water, though she knew it was there, hundreds of feet below. The sensation was like driving at the edge of the world.

Once they were inland the sun came out. Darien felt better, but she was beginning to get nervous, knowing she'd soon have to tell him she wouldn't see him again.

When they came through the Rainbow Tunnel and San Francisco was spread out before them across the Golden Gate, Darien decided the time had come. "Sam," she said, "I need to talk to you about next weekend."

"Yes?"

"I respect you enough that I feel I should be direct."

He gave her a wary look. "Bad news has a distinctive sound," he said. "What's the matter?"

"The past few weekends have been among the most enjoyable of my life. You're a wonderful lover. You bring new meaning to the word fantasy. Even without knowing you, I like you. But I don't think I should see you again."

He was silent for a moment. "I was with you right up to the last sentence. Why not, Darien?"

"It has nothing to do with you," she said. "You've been terrific. But even the best fantasies must end, and I want this one to stop while it's still good."

"Forgive me, but that's the stupidest thing I've ever heard. By that logic we should all commit suicide because we'll die eventually, anyway."

She took a deep breath. "I'm trying to explain as best I can. Feelings can't always be expressed clearly. And you'll just have to accept that this is the way I feel."

They had come to the bridge and started across the span. Darien glanced at the ocean, but couldn't see much because of a fog bank lying beyond the headlands. She had a sick feeling. This was proving to be a lot more difficult than she'd expected.

"May I ask what happened to make you decide you don't want to play anymore?" he asked.

She turned to him. "Nothing *happened*, Sam. The game has run its course, that's all."

"I don't buy it," he said. "There's something else, and I'd like to understand what it is, if that isn't asking too much."

"It's over, that's all."

They came to the tollbooth and Sam handed the toll keeper three dollars. They drove through.

"You're afraid of something," he said, "and it's apparently me. What I don't understand is what I did to offend you. Was it coming to your place unannounced the other night? Did I frighten you?"

"No."

"Then what?"

"It doesn't matter. It was a game. We played it. The clock has run out."

"Well, you're certainly within your rights to say that," he said, flushing, "but I'd like to think I'm deserving of a little consideration."

"What do you expect of me?" she demanded, her voice growing shrill. "What else do I owe you?"

He glanced at her, then at the road. "How about a chance to get beyond the fantasy? I was Sam for you. Now why can't I be myself?"

"Because I don't want that!"

"The notion's that offensive, huh?"

"I told you it has nothing to do with you."

"You're just stonewalling, Darien," he said with disgust.

She was silent for a moment. "I was hoping you'd understand."

"Well, now I do. The game has run its course. You got what you wanted. After all, how many times can a person write about a sexy weekend with a stranger?"

He was bitter and she could hardly blame him. He'd invested a lot in this. On the other hand, she'd made no promises. They had both understood the ground rules.

"I've been thinking about it," she said, "and I want us to split the cost of our trips. It's not fair that you carry the entire financial burden."

"Oh, I've received fair value," he replied caustically. "Besides, it's no burden. I'll just content myself with the thought that I've contributed to the progress of journalism in the Bay Area."

"You don't have to be sarcastic."

"No, you're right," he said. "A deal is a deal."

She couldn't tell if he was trying to make her feel bad, or if he was trying to be reasonable and mature. Either way, what could she do? Telling him had been a hell of a lot kinder than pretending everything was fine and then standing him up when he invited her on another fantasy.

Nothing more was said until they pulled up in front of her place. "Well, here we are," he said, turning off the engine.

Darien returned the Hermés scarf to the glove box. She looked at him, feeling embarrassed and sad. She'd steeled herself against this, purposely trying to keep it from becoming an emotional issue. "I can't begin to tell you how grateful I am," she said tentatively.

"There's no need for thanks."

"No, I do want to thank you, Sam. You could have taken advantage of me. I took a big risk getting involved with you, but you made it all right."

"I'm glad to hear that," he said with a twinge of irony.

"I'm referring to the fact that you were a gentleman and respected our agreement. You already know how I feel about the experience. It's been a wonderful fantasy. A fantastic one."

He contemplated her. "It never got beyond that with you, did it? It was just grist for the journalistic mill."

"That was the whole purpose."

His expression betrayed his disappointment. "At least you're honest. I have to admire your integrity, I suppose."

"After Las Vegas I considered ending it. I should have. It was a mistake not to."

He gazed up the street, shaking his head. "They say men are the sentimental ones. I didn't truly understand that until now."

"This isn't easy for me, either," she said. "But I'm trying to be reasonable."

"Are you suggesting that I'm not?" he shot back.

"No, of course not."

"Well, maybe I let myself get more emotional than I had a right to. I let myself care about you, forgetting it was only a game. I regret that. It wasn't part of our deal."

She lowered her head. "That wasn't supposed to happen," she said softly.

"I didn't intend it, either. But what's the expression? The road to hell is paved with good intentions?"

"I feel terrible," she said.

"Don't. I'm a big boy. I went into this with my eyes open. I just outsmarted myself, that's all." He reached over and took her hand. "Hoist by my own petard."

"It has nothing to do with you," she said, a sheen of tears filming her eyes. "Honestly, Sam."

"I know. It was business. My mistake was thinking of it as personal. But don't worry. I'm not headed for the Golden Gate Bridge. What is, is."

"That's not what I meant. I didn't *want* to feel anything for you."

"That's obvious."

"I could have," she snapped, "but I didn't want to."

"Darien, your willpower is admirable. You're to be congratulated."

"Oh, don't be so damned snide. I'm trying to explain that you couldn't possibly understand my reasons for ending this. I could have gotten emotionally involved if I let myself. I just couldn't let this go on!"

She was shaking with emotion, her cheeks coloring. She drew a ragged breath, wondering why in the hell she kept trying to explain herself when there was nothing to be gained by it.

"Why?" he said.

"Why what?"

"*Why* couldn't you let this go on? What are you afraid of? Me?"

"No. Not you."

"Then what?"

"For God's sake, Sam. All I wanted was a fantasy. Can't we leave it at that?"

"No. I think what happened between us meant more to you than you're willing to admit. You've been fighting me . . . almost from the first. What harm would it do to give me a chance? The men in your fantasies are perfect by definition, I understand that. I'm not perfect. Maybe I'd fall short of your standards, but why reject me without getting to know me?"

Darien felt like everything was closing in on her. She couldn't take any more. She opened the door and got out of the car. "Please get my suitcase out of the trunk," she said, forcing herself to be calm. "I want to go in now."

"All right, dammit," he said, opening the door, "but my name is not Sam. It's Stephen. Sam is dead as far as I'm concerned." He opened the trunk and took out her bag. "And you can put that in your next article. Sam Smith is dead. Died right along with your fantasy. He drove off a cliff, jumped off the bridge . . . say whatever you want. But if you're going to say goodbye, at least say goodbye to *me*, not some fictional character you tried to put in my skin." He set her suitcase on the sidewalk and dusted off his hands.

Darien was sure she was going to break into tears. "The last thing I wanted to do was hurt you."

"Forget it," he said. "No hard feelings. As long as you know how I feel about you, I can't complain." He extended his hand. "Maybe the problem was it was a little too good." He smiled wryly. "I won't make that mistake again."

Her eyes welled as she shook his hand. "Maybe it was a little too good for me, too," she whispered. She picked up her suitcase.

"Let me carry that for you," he said.

Darien shook her head. "No, I'll do it." She bit her lip, but she couldn't keep the tears from overflowing. She wiped them away with the back of her hand. "You'd better go before I cry."

He suddenly looked terribly sad. Darien felt certain her heart would break. She stepped forward, kissed his cheek, then spun and practically ran around the house, not stopping until she got to the door of her cottage. As she fumbled with her keys, she heard the engine of the MG roar to life. She could hear the car going up the street until the sound finally faded. He was gone. Sam—no, it was Stephen—was gone. For good.

IT WAS a rotten evening. Darien sat on the nubby white sofa in her front room, filled with second thoughts. Poor Sam—Stephen—didn't know what hit him. One minute she was in bed with him, making love, the next it was goodbye.

He'd been more upset than she'd anticipated. But how was she to know his feelings were so strong? He hadn't said anything until then to indicate he cared. Of course, she hadn't exactly given him much of a chance.

Darien got up from the sofa and went to the window to look into the garden. Twilight was rapidly approaching. Why did she feel so empty? In the past, the end of a relationship would come as a relief. It was sometimes painful, even sad, but always a relief. This time it wasn't.

When the telephone rang, she turned from the window and hurried to answer it. Her first thought was that it was Sam—no, Stephen. How would she ever get that straight? Sam was a fantasy man. Stephen was real.

"Hello?" she said expectantly.

"Darien?" It was her mother, a voice so familiar, yet unexpected.

"Hi, Mom."

"Am I calling at a bad time?"

"No, I was just sitting here thinking." Then it occurred to her that she didn't often hear from her parents unless there was a special reason. "Is everything all right?" she asked warily.

"Yes, yes," her mother said, "I just thought since it was a Sunday evening, I'd telephone. We're down on the Cape, you know. Your father and I were talking about you at dinner and I decided why not give you a call?"

"It's a nice surprise," she said, unsure what her mother was up to.

"There isn't any news is there, Darien?"

"News? What sort of news?"

"Well, anything special happening in your life?"

"Mother, why are you being so coy? This is a very strange phone call."

She heard her mother sigh. "Maybe I should be more direct. Your father and I were wondering about Sam. Is he real and as wonderful as you make out, or is it all journalistic hyperbole?"

Darien couldn't believe her ears. "How on earth do you know about Sam?"

"Your father gave me a subscription to your paper for Mother's Day. He thought it would be a good way to keep up with your career. You're really a marvelous writer, dear. And these articles about Sam are . . . well, captivating."

Darien felt the color rising in her cheeks. "I can't tell you what a surprise this is. Somehow I didn't picture you and Dad reading those articles."

"Oh, my, I hope that isn't a problem for you."

"No, to tell you the truth I'm kind of flattered. I didn't think you cared that much about my work, that's all."

"Of course we care about it. Just because we aren't on the phone all the time doesn't mean we don't care, Darien. You're an adult and we try to respect your privacy. We know you have a life of your own and there are things to which we are not privy."

"Apparently your curiosity got the best of you on this, though," Darien said.

"Well, yes. To be honest, we were curious about this man, if he's . . . well, real."

"He's real, all right, but he's just passing through my life. He's just someone I wrote about."

"Oh, that's too bad. This is the first man you've shown much passion for since Todd—that we've been aware of, anyway. We took that to be a good sign."

"What do you mean by passion, Mother?"

"Your feelings came out in your writing loud and clear. It was the particulars we were unsure of. Personally, I couldn't have imagined you making it up, but your father wasn't so sure."

"I didn't make it up," Darien said, feeling that emptiness again. How bizarre—to be discussing this with her mother, of all people.

"You know what I was reminded of?" Alice Hughes said.

"What?"

"You're going to hate me for saying this, but I couldn't help thinking of that game of pretend you always played as a child."

"What game of pretend, Mother?"

"Don't you remember, dear? You had that imaginary little playmate, I believe his name was Harry or Larry, something like that. You used to play up in your room, babbling away, carrying on a conversation with him by the hour."

"Yes, now that you mention it I do remember Larry. Some of it's coming back."

"I felt so guilty," her mother went on. "I was afraid you had a developmental problem because you were so attached to your friend. So one day I told you I thought you spent too much time with Larry, that you ought to seek out real live children. You were crushed. You never talked about your little friend again.

"Later on, I happened to mention the incident to the head of the psychology department and she told me that imaginary play was entirely normal. And then I worried that I might have harmed you with my meddling, stifled you, perhaps."

"Mother, I can scarcely remember any of what you're talking about. If I was traumatized, the effects have long passed."

"Well, I admit I'd halfway forgotten about it myself until I read about Sam. Then it all came back. After all, he is a sort of playmate, as well."

Darien was glad her mother wasn't there to see the color rising in her face.

"I am pleased to hear you didn't make it all up, though," her mother went on. "He seemed like such a . . . well, in my day we'd have said quite a man."

"He was."

There was a pause on the line. "No real-life possibilities of anything coming of it, then?"

"No, Mother."

"Oh, well, I admit I'm a little disappointed." She sighed. "Perhaps your father and I are just getting to that age."

"What age?"

"Grandparents. We made our parents grandparents, you know, and assumed the same would happen to us one day."

Darien couldn't help wondering what had gotten into her mother. She'd known her accounts of Sam had been moving, even inspiring for a number of people. But her own parents, all the way back in Massachusetts? "I'm afraid there's a big step from writing about a man to getting impregnated by him," she said.

Her mother cleared her throat. "Judging by your enthusiasm for your subject, I wouldn't think quite so far as you make it sound."

Darien gulped.

"Well, I've tormented you enough about Sam," her mother said. "The last thing I want to do with him is what I did with Larry." She laughed to let her know she wasn't entirely serious. "So tell me, dear, any other news?"

"No," Darien said, "not really. What's new with you and Dad?"

"We're having a lovely time on the Cape. But then we always do. We've got the cottage for three more weeks. If you feel you can get away, we'd love to have you come and join us."

"Thanks, Mom, but I don't have any vacation time yet. Maybe next year. We'll have to talk about it."

"Yes, by all means. I'd put your father on, but he ran down to the market for some milk. I probably should have waited until he was back, but the urge struck and so I picked up the phone."

"I'm glad you did."

"Well, keep up the good work, dear. You're a good writer. I do very much enjoy reading your pieces."

"Thanks, Mom. I appreciate you saying that."

Darien hung up the phone in a mild state of shock. She wouldn't have imagined having that conversation in a hundred years.

Sam seemed to have affected a far broader spectrum of her life than she would have imagined. He'd even managed to dig up an old skeleton from the family closet. Larry. It had been years and years since that business of her imaginary friend had so much as crossed her mind.

She smiled at the thought. Maybe Larry and Sam weren't so different, when you came right down to it. There was an awful lot that was imaginary about a fantasy lover. But in Sam's—Stephen's—case, an awful lot that was real, as well. Of course, it was all in the past now. He was gone. She'd sent him on his way and she still wasn't a hundred percent sure why.

14

DARIEN CALLED Maryanne on Monday morning to see if she had plans for lunch. Maryanne suggested that they meet at the Vailancourt fountain. They often met there at lunchtime to have a sandwich on the grass and watch the people.

"What do you make of it?" Darien said, after she'd related the events of the weekend. "Am I a neurotic, a psychotic or just plain confused?"

Maryanne pushed her windblown hair out of her face and stared at the fountain. She was chewing and took her time before responding. "What you did is not so important as how you feel about it," she said.

That seemed to Darien to be a reasonable observation, though not a very helpful one. "That's the problem. I don't *know* how I feel about it."

"You have doubts. You're second-guessing yourself."

"Obviously. But what choice do I have? No one in their right mind would base a decision about their emotional life on the fact that they've discovered great sex. That's just not a good enough reason to continue a relationship. Besides, the sex was a little too good. I didn't want to get anymore addicted than I already was."

Maryanne grinned. "Ah, I understand. You're saying you wanted something else from Sam. Besides the sex."

"No," she said lightly, "that was all I wanted. And I thought it was all he wanted, too."

Maryanne stopped to run the logic of that through her mind, scratching her head. "I'm afraid you're losing me, kiddo. Let's try this a different way. What do you want at this point?"

"I don't know."

"All right, then. What are you afraid of?"

Darien thought. "I'm not sure. Making a mistake, I guess."

"What kind of mistake?"

Darien closed her eyes, knowing that to answer that question was to face her demons. "I guess...I guess when you come right down to it I'm..."

"You're what?"

"Afraid I'll get hurt. That something awful might happen."

Maryanne chomped on her sandwich, taking a swig from her juice bottle between bites. "Any idea why?"

Darien lowered her eyes. "Todd," she said. It was barely a whisper. A gust of wind came up, blowing a fine mist from the fountain in their direction. She looked up as her eyes welled.

"Could it be that you don't want to love anybody for fear of losing them and being hurt again?" Maryanne said. "Sam was safe because he was pretend, your own creation."

"Just like Larry," Darien said absently.

"Who?"

She told Maryanne about her imaginary childhood friend and her conversation with her mother. "You know, I hardly gave it much thought last night when she called, except to be surprised that she had been carrying something like that with her all these years. But afterward I dreamed about my parents. And about Larry and Stephen and God knows what else."

"Was it an anxious dream?"

"No. But when I woke up I realized all wasn't well with the world. I had an empty feeling in the pit of my stomach."

Maryanne finished her sandwich. "This might sound strange, but I don't think you're as confused as you sound. I think you know exactly what's wrong, but you don't want to face up to it."

Darien stared off for a long time, thinking about the Sam she knew, the Stephen she didn't know. "I suppose you're right. I regret that I was too scared to give Stephen a chance."

"I don't like to play therapist with my friends," Maryanne said, "but I think you've been a prisoner of your past for a long time—ever since Todd died—and now you've found someone you care enough about to escape, but you're having trouble acting on those feelings. You're trying to run from them and that doesn't work."

"You're right. I'm afraid. I don't want to go through what I went through with Todd."

"There are two ways to deal with it. You can hide or you can confront your fears."

"Easier said than done," Darien said.

"If it was easy, kiddo, I'd be out of business."

"So what do I do?"

"You tried running and something inside you is giving you a lot of grief for that decision. Maybe you need to try the other course—be honest with Stephen. If he's as understanding as you say, maybe he can help. The first step toward an intimate relationship is honest communication.

"Stephen doesn't want to be Sam anymore. Presumably that means he wants you to appreciate him for who he really is. It's important you let him know who you really are, too, Darien. Your fears are as important as your fantasies, because they are part of you, too. We're all the sum of our parts. The good, the bad, strengths, weaknesses, virtues and faults."

Darien looked into her friend's eyes. "Has anybody nominated you for the Nobel Prize?"

"Hell, I'm lucky if I have a date on a Saturday night."

Darien gave her a hug. "You know, there's only one thing wrong."

"What's that?"

"The last time I saw Stephen he was driving off into the sunset. I don't even know his last name. Even if I knew how to get hold of him, there's no guarantee he'd talk to me."

"Fear of failure," Maryanne said flatly.

"Well, if you're so smart, what would *you* do?"

Maryanne pushed her hair out of her face and thought. "Sam found you the first time because he read your article. Maybe you can get to Stephen the same way."

"Hmm," Darien said, considering the remark. "I was having trouble coming up with a hook for my next piece. Maybe this is it! Now all I have to do is figure out how to let Stephen know I want a second chance."

OVER THE COURSE of the afternoon they drifted by her cubicle—Bob Smits, Rod Barker, Virginia and two or three others. They were all were curious about her weekend. Only Virginia found the courage to ask.

"You can read about it in the *Bulletin*," Darien said without looking up from her computer. "It'll be in tomorrow's edition."

Word got around that something was up. There were whispers in every corner. Darien couldn't be sure what they were saying, but if it was like most gossip, there'd be speculation ranging from the notion that Sam had asked her to marry him all the way to she'd discovered he was a transvestite and ended up dumping him. At this point she didn't care what people were thinking, she had a clear-cut mission—to reach out to Stephen.

She wrote for two hours before she stopped to scroll back over the last few paragraphs she'd written.

As we drove through Marin, I looked at Sam. I'd spent the most fantastic weekends of my life with him, yet in spite of all we'd shared I felt discontented. And I didn't understand why.

I knew he was planning another marvelous adventure for us, but suddenly I realized all my fantasies had been fulfilled, except one. Sam hadn't revealed himself to me, not the person he truly was. And that was only because I had stopped him.

When we pulled up in front of my place, Sam turned off the engine of the MG and said, "I haven't come up with a plan for next week yet. Do you have another secret fantasy?"

Sam was giving me the chance I needed. "There's only one thing left that matters," I told him. "Discovering who you really are . . . assuming you're willing to share the truth."

Sam looked me in the eye and said, "This is your fantasy, Darien, the night games have all been for you. It's up to you to say what happens next."

"It's time for this adventure to end," I said. "When I get out of the car, it will be the last time I see you. But next Saturday afternoon at three o'clock I'm going back to Tiburon to hang out on the deck at Sam's. I'm hoping I'll see a very special man there, just as I did last time. Only this time it will be dif-

ferent. I'm going to sit down at his table and introduce myself. And if he's interested in getting to know
me, I'll buy him a drink and ask him to tell me about
his life. I'll want to learn everything about him—his
strengths and weaknesses, his virtues and faults. I'll
want to know about the good as well as the bad.
Fantasies can be wonderful, but in the long run the
truth, real life, is all that counts."

It was a difficult thing to say after all the magical
hours we'd spent together but I knew I was doing
was the right thing. In my heart, I believe Sam knew
that even better than I.

I'm not sure what next weekend will bring. I won't
ever see Sam again, that much is certain. But I'll be
in Tiburon Saturday, hoping I'll encounter that
special someone who's identity I don't yet know.
But if he—let's call him Stephen—shows up and is
willing to give me a chance, then I promise to do the
same for him.

A wise man once said we have nothing to fear but
fear itself. I've come to realize that bit of wisdom is
especially true in my life. I can only hope this new
insight has not come too late to make the most important dream of all a reality.

SATURDAY was a glorious day. Sunlight sparkled on the
bay. Sailboats dotted the blue green water from Fort
Point to Angel Island. Darien had gone to Marina Park
early that morning to walk along the promenade and fill
her lungs with that brisk ocean air blowing through the
Golden Gate. She hadn't slept at all well for a couple of
days and needed to do something to clear the cobwebs
from her brain.

She got back to her place mid-morning and found Marc sitting in the garden, having a cup of espresso he'd made with the machine Dean had given him for Christmas.

"I was wondering where you were," he said with a smile. "No sign of life in the cottage."

"I'm not sure that will change much now that I'm home."

Marc looked sympathetic. "Nervous, sweetie?"

"I'm a zombie," she said.

"No calls? Never heard from him?"

"Not a word."

"I wouldn't take that as a sign of anything. No news is good news. I believe that," he said. "Honestly."

"I hope you're right."

"What are you wearing?"

"I haven't decided," she said woefully.

"What did you wear the first time you went to Sam's?"

"A sleeveless yellow T-shirt dress."

Marc considered that. "Hmm. I think you should wear it again."

"Why?"

"For psychological reasons. And for luck."

"You think I'll need it?"

"With your face? You won't *need* it, exactly."

"Then—"

"Sweetie, in matters of romance, never leave anything to chance. This is a big day. Fire every weapon, use every trick, don't hold anything back."

She shook her head. "You know, it really doesn't matter what I wear, Marc. He'll either be there or he won't. That'll be the whole ball game."

"Wear the yellow dress. Trust me."

Darien sighed. If Marc had told her to throw salt over her shoulder or pin a four-leaf clover to her underwear, she'd have done it. At this point, fate had complete control and she was just along for the ride. "I'll wear the yellow dress," she said.

Marc gave her thumbs up, and she went inside to get ready for the drive up to Tiburon. Maryanne had loaned Darien her car. She'd also offered to go along, if Darien felt she needed the moral support, but she'd declined. "If he doesn't show up, I'd prefer to endure my misery alone."

For lunch she had a carrot, a piece of whole grain bread and a glass of apple juice. She didn't think she'd be able to keep down anything heavier. The extent of her anxiety surprised her. She'd tried to prepare herself, to put things into some kind of perspective. But with each passing hour, the tension seemed to build. The worst that could happen, she told herself, was that he wouldn't be there. The world wouldn't end. She'd keep on breathing. She might even run into him again down the line.

Sound as the reasoning was, she didn't buy it. It seemed like the entire course of her life was dependent upon what was waiting for her on the deck of Sam's.

Forty-five minutes was long enough to get to Tiburon, but Darien left the house at two anyway, in order to allow herself a little extra time. She clutched the wheel of Maryanne's Mustang tightly as she drove to Marin, hating herself for having gotten into this situation to begin with. Maryanne had put the top up so Darien's hair wouldn't be a mess by the time she got there, but that hardly seemed important now. The only thing that mattered was how much Stephen cared for her and how understanding and forgiving he was.

There seemed to be a number of cars exiting the freeway at Tiburon Boulevard. Saturdays in the summer were big days in the quaint, picturesque spots of Marin, especially when the weather was good. Still, the traffic was heavier than she'd expected. When the flow slowed to a crawl, Darien started to worry. What was wrong? she wondered. Was there an accident?

For ten minutes the traffic inched along. It seemed as if everybody was going into Tiburon. Just her luck. The whole damn world decided to go to Marin on the day she was trying to undo the biggest screw-up of her life.

Suddenly a thought hit her. This congestion couldn't be because of her, could it? In order to let Stephen know she was going to be at Sam's at three o'clock on Saturday, she'd had to tell a couple of million other people. It hadn't occurred to her that she might draw a curious crowd. Nobody knew what she—or Stephen—looked like, but maybe there were a number of people who just wanted to hang around where the big event was to take place. Now that she thought about it, it could make for idle sport, perhaps even a festive occasion. Lord, that's probably what this traffic was all about.

She checked her watch. It was a quarter to, and she was a mile from the village. At this rate, she'd never make it. Wouldn't that be ironic—missing Stephen because she couldn't get through the traffic jam she'd caused by publicizing the event!

Soon a police officer came walking down the lane of traffic, speaking to the drivers. "You might want to consider turning around," he told her. "The municipal lots are all full."

"What's going on, Officer?" she asked.

"Some media event at Sam's. Apparently you aren't one of the gawkers."

"No, but I do need to get into town."

"Your chances are better on foot," the officer said before moving on.

Darien noticed that a few cars ahead were starting to turn around, others continued to wait. The short stretches where parking was allowed were already filled, so she simply pulled as far off the pavement as she could and turned off the engine. It would probably mean a ticket, but she didn't care.

Grabbing her purse, she jumped out of the car and began hurrying along the bicycle path that traced the water's edge. Others were doing the same and Darien joined the stream of humanity, headed to Sam's to witness what was supposed to be her moment of truth.

"He's supposed to be real good-looking," one teenage girl tromping along was saying to another, "so she probably is, too."

"I bet it's all a hoax," the other replied.

Darien consulted her watch again, realizing she was going to be late. Would Sam wait? Would he even be there?

Her heart pounded. She began to run, dodging around people who were themselves hurrying. If these were the late arrivals, she thought, what sort of crowd was waiting at the restaurant?

She arrived in Tiburon, breathless. The police had cordoned off Main, the narrow little street where Sam's was located. To her amazement there was a TV news truck parked at the far end of the street. A camera crew was working the crowd. There was a carnival atmosphere. People were milling about the street, but nobody seemed to know quite what they were looking for.

The crowd was even thicker at the entrance to Sam's. People were pressed to the door. Darien groaned. Here she was, stuck in her own trap. But she couldn't give up now.

It was obvious they weren't allowing anyone else inside unless somebody left. She pushed her way through the crowd, raising the ire of those she elbowed aside. Finally, hot and sweaty from her run and the struggle to get to the door, she made it to the front. Two large men were guarding the entrance, acting as bouncers.

"I've got to get inside," she pleaded.

"You and everybody else, lady," one of them said to her.

"Wait your turn!" somebody behind her shouted.

"Look," she said to the beefy man blocking the way, "I'm Darien Hughes."

"Honey, you're the fifteenth one so far."

"I've got a driver's license and a press card to prove it," she said breathlessly.

He gave her a skeptical look. "Yeah? Let's see 'em."

Fumbling through her purse, she pulled out her wallet and showed the bouncer her license and press card.

"Well, what do you know," he said.

"Hey, it's her!" somebody said.

"It's the writer. It's Darien," another voice echoed.

Soon the mob was rumbling. The bouncer took Darien by the arm and passed her to his cohort, who allowed her to slip inside. The bar was jam-packed, and the second bouncer, who was right behind her, pushed past her, leading the way toward the deck, where another pair of bouncers was guarding the rear doorway.

"Got the real one this time," her escort said.

"Hallelujah," one of the others replied.

Again a murmur went through the crowd and people began pressing forward. One of the men opened the door for her and stepped out with her onto the ramp that led from the restaurant to the deck area.

Darien was shocked. The deck was empty! No crowds, no diners or staff, just a bunch of tables and chairs. "What happened?" she asked.

"The gentleman rented the entire deck for the afternoon," the bouncer said, pointing.

Then she saw him, seated at the far corner of the deck, at the very same table he'd been at that first day. It was Stephen, dressed as he had been when he'd first become her fantasy man. Her heart began to race. Her rosy cheeks turned a deeper crimson.

Darien stared at him, suddenly self-conscious, aware she looked hot and disheveled. But there was no helping that now. She made her way down the ramp and stepped onto the deck.

Stephen was looking off, waiting, just as he had that day. But this time, *she* was the one he was waiting for. She made her way around the deck. It was strangely quiet. Mainly she heard the gulls cawing as they soared above the marina.

Stephen turned as he saw her approach. He slowly got to his feet. Darien stopped in front of him.

"Hi," she said.

"Hello."

She extended her hand. "I'm Darien Hughes."

"Stephen Royden," he said, gripping her hand firmly. "Would you care to join me?"

Stephen Royden, she thought. Why did that name sound familiar? "Thank you," she said, as he seated her. Were there Roydens in Boston she should know? she wondered. Probably, but she couldn't make the connection.

He returned to his chair. "Lovely day," he said, looking out at the naked masks of the sailboats.

"It *is* pretty. And quiet."

"Quiet makes for more intimate conversation," he said.

Darien glanced toward the building. Dozens of faces were in the big picture windows overlooking the deck. The windows of the adjacent buildings were filled with onlookers, as well. A few young men were perched on nearby rooftops.

"So, you're a writer," he said. "A very popular one, by all indications."

"I think the secret of my success is that I may appeal to people's prurient interests. How about you, Stephen?"

"I don't know if that's the aspect of you that appeals to me the most or not, but the appeal is indisputable."

She blushed. "No. I mean, what do you do?"

"Venture capital," he said. "Mostly high-tech investments. Computer games, that sort of thing."

"I see." She paused. "Are you from Boston?"

"Originally. I've been out here a year or so. I had so many clients down in the Silicon Valley, and was out here so much, I decided I might as well live nearby."

"Your name is familiar, but I can't quite place it. Are you from a prominent family?"

"My father and grandfather were successful businessmen, if that's what you mean. It's a well-known name back east."

"I see," she said. She glanced around, feeling like she was in a fishbowl.

"Is that a problem?" he asked.

"No, of course not. I just couldn't place it . . . and as I said, it sounded familiar."

Then Darien anxiously looked down at the table for a moment. She took a deep breath and met Stephen's curious gaze. "Do you think we could be friends? Of the normal variety, I mean?"

"Hey, Ms. Hughes, I don't plan on tossing the baby out with the bath water. A little imagination and a sense of adventure are good for any relationship. I don't plan on changing."

"But that wasn't you, Stephen."

"Oh? Are you sure?"

"You mean . . . you're really . . ."

"Yes, that's exactly what I mean. The only thing wrong with that picture was the true identity of the man you were with. I have a hunch you can handle knowing the driver's license in my wallet says Stephen Royden, not Sam Smith." He squeezed her fingers. "The guy you're looking at, Darien, plays a little baccarat from time to time. He likes quiet weekends up the coast. He's capable of surprising you in the middle of the night. And I may even have a few more tricks up my sleeve you haven't discovered yet."

Darien turned red and glanced at the growing crowd on the nearby rooftops. Then she looked into his eyes again.

"All I want to be is who I am," he said. "The rest is unimportant. The question, the *only* question, is if you can accept me on that basis."

"I know it was my idea to come here, but I feel like I'm in a fishbowl."

He pointed into the marina. "See that little cabin cruiser moored to the far dock?" he said.

"Yes."

"I borrowed it for the day. There's a chilled bottle of champagne aboard, and I know a quiet cove where we can drop anchor."

She gave him a smile. "You certainly believe in planning ahead, don't you . . . Stephen?"

"I was hoping we'd have something to celebrate." Reaching across the table, he touched her cheek. Then he drew it to his mouth and kissed her fingers.

There was a loud whistle from a nearby rooftop, then some applause. She looked at the crowd anxiously.

"Maybe we should take that cruise sooner rather than later," she said, getting up from her chair.

"I was never one to make a public display," he said. In one smooth motion he rose, took her hand and drew her into his arms. "But maybe, since they went to such trouble to get here, we ought to give them a little something for their money."

Darien looked at him. "Like what?"

Leaning down, he kissed her, holding her tight. She began to kiss him back, losing herself in the moment. She hardly heard the cheer go up or the cawing of the gulls. The balmy breeze, the warm sunshine—they all faded away. But when the kiss ended they weren't alone any longer.

"Maybe it's time to go," he whispered in her ear.

Slipping his wallet from his pocket, he removed a hundred-dollar bill and left it on the table. Then, taking her hand, they exited the deck and made their way out through the marina toward the cabin cruiser.

"Stephen, can I ask you something? And I don't mean something that can be answered yes or no."

"Sure," he said with a smile. "Ask anything you want."

"What would you have done if I hadn't written that last article saying I'd be here today, hoping you'd come?"

"I don't know. Maybe bought a piece of the *Bulletin* and asked you to write the article, or one like it."

"You weren't planning on fading away, then?"

They'd come to the boat. Stephen stopped, took her hands and looked into her eyes. "My love, you're about to discover that the fantasies have been mine every bit as much as they've been yours. The only difference is my version always ends happily." He kissed her. "And from now on, yours will, too."

HARLEQUIN®
Temptation®

Secret Fantasies

Do you have a secret fantasy?

Carol Glendower does. More than anything, she wants her husband back. Evan was handsome, sexy…perfect. But he's gone, and she's alone. Carol will have to risk *everything* to fulfill her fantasy. Dare she?

Find out in #534 THE TEMPTING by Lisa Harris, available in April 1995.

Everybody has a secret fantasy. And you'll find them all in Temptation's exciting new yearlong miniseries, Secret Fantasies. Beginning January 1995, one book each month focuses on the hero or heroine's innermost romantic fantasy.…

HARLEQUIN®

PRESENTS
RELUCTANT BRIDEGROOMS

Two beautiful brides, two unforgettable romances...
two men running for their lives....

My Lady Love, by Paula Marshall, introduces
Charles, Viscount Halstead, who lost his memory
and found himself employed as a stableboy by the
untouchable Nell Tallboys, Countess Malplaquet.
But Nell didn't consider Charles untouchable—
not at all!

Darling Amazon, by Sylvia Andrew, is the story of
a spurious engagement between Julia Marchant
and Hugo, marquess of Rostherne—an engagement
that gets out of hand and just may lead Hugo to
the altar after all!

Enjoy two madcap Regency weddings this May,
wherever Harlequin books are sold.

REG5

MOVE OVER, MELROSE PLACE!

Come live and love in L.A. with the tenants of Bachelor Arms. Enjoy a year's worth of wonderful love stories and meet colorful neighbors you'll bump into again and again.

First, we'll introduce you to Bachelor Arms residents Josh, Tru and Garrett—three to-die-for and determined bachelor buddies—who do everything they can to avoid walking down the aisle. Bestselling author Kate Hoffmann brings us these romantic comedies in the new continuity series from Temptation.

A HAPPILY UNMARRIED MAN #533 (April 1995)

Soon to move into Bachelor Arms are the heroes and heroines in books by our most popular authors— JoAnn Ross, Candace Schuler and Judith Arnold. You'll read a new book every month.

Don't miss the goings-on at Bachelor Arms.

Harlequin invites you to the most
romantic wedding of the season.

Rope the cowboy of your dreams in
Marry Me, Cowboy!

A collection of 4 brand-new stories,
celebrating weddings, written by:

New York Times bestselling author

JANET DAILEY

and favorite authors

Margaret Way
Anne McAllister
Susan Fox

Be sure not to miss Marry Me, Cowboy!
coming this April

HARLEQUIN®

Don't miss these Harlequin favorites by some of our most
distinguished authors!
And now, you can receive a discount by ordering two or more titles!

HT#25577	WILD LIKE THE WIND by Janice Kaiser	$2.99	☐
HT#25589	THE RETURN OF CAINE O'HALLORAN by JoAnn Ross	$2.99	☐
HP#11626	THE SEDUCTION STAKES by Lindsay Armstrong	$2.99	☐
HP#11647	GIVE A MAN A BAD NAME by Roberta Leigh	$2.99	☐
HR#03293	THE MAN WHO CAME FOR CHRISTMAS by Bethany Campbell	$2.89	☐
HR#03308	RELATIVE VALUES by Jessica Steele	$2.89	☐
SR#70589	CANDY KISSES by Muriel Jensen	$3.50	☐
SR#70598	WEDDING INVITATION by Marisa Carroll	$3.50 U.S. $3.99 CAN.	☐ ☐
HI#22230	CACHE POOR by Margaret St. George	$2.99	☐
HAR#16515	NO ROOM AT THE INN by Linda Randall Wisdom	$3.50	☐
HAR#16520	THE ADVENTURESS by M.J. Rodgers	$3.50	☐
HS#28795	PIECES OF SKY by Marianne Willman	$3.99	☐
HS#28824	A WARRIOR'S WAY by Margaret Moore	$3.99 U.S. $4.50 CAN.	☐ ☐

(limited quantities available on certain titles)

	AMOUNT	$
DEDUCT:	**10% DISCOUNT FOR 2+ BOOKS**	$
ADD:	**POSTAGE & HANDLING**	$
	($1.00 for one book, 50¢ for each additional)	
	APPLICABLE TAXES*	$_____
	TOTAL PAYABLE	$_____
	(check or money order—please do not send cash)	

To order, complete this form and send it, along with a check or money order for the
total above, payable to Harlequin Books, to: **In the U.S.:** 3010 Walden Avenue,
P.O. Box 9047, Buffalo, NY 14269-9047; **In Canada:** P.O. Box 613, Fort Erie, Ontario,
L2A 5X3.

Name: _____

Address: _____ City: _____

State/Prov.: _____ Zip/Postal Code: _____

*New York residents remit applicable sales taxes.
 Canadian residents remit applicable GST and provincial taxes.

HBACK-JM2